WHISPERS FROM BEFORE

TALES OF MYTH AND LEGEND

ROSIE GRYMM   HANNAH CARTER   ABIGAIL MCKENNA

MARIELLA TAYLOR   SAVANNA ROBERTS

PRESS

Printed in the United States of America

ISBN: 979-8-7539822-1-6

Beneath a harvest moon,
blood red and rising,
when no one else will listen
and you stand alone with shadows,
searching the darkness
for a kindred ear, a soul mate—
peel back the purple night and see
that the nymphs in the grasses
and sprites in the hollows
are standing up on tiptoe,
listening.

Leave your manufactured cage
and follow the serpent's trail
that warps through the forest
to where the fire faerie dance
around a florescent fire,
spinning tales
about the Goblin King
and his ghost-gray mountain.
Take out your ember pen,
let it set fire to the page
and burn into your soul
forever.

Write it out on the sky,
where the lava sun
sets in the heavens.
Let it thunder in your ears
like beating drums in the desert
and echo in your heart
where no one ever visits.
Pour it out on paper,
let it bleed into the ink,
and burn into your soul
forever.

"Sky Paper" By Savannah Jezowski. Previously published in *For Love of a Word*

WHISPERS FROM BEFORE

TALES OF MYTH AND LEGEND

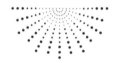

ROSIE GRYMM   HANNAH CARTER   ABIGAIL MCKENNA

MARIELLA TAYLOR   SAVANNA ROBERTS

PRESS

THE GUMIHO OF DRAGON RIVER

BY ROSIE GRYMM

There was blood on my hands. It dripped from my fingers and splattered the pale skirt of my hanbok, like fireworks in a clear sky. The rain outside pounded a loud rhythm in my head and that was all I could think about, nothing but the noise and the chill it brought to a summer night.

With my foot, I nudged the crumpled body on the floor; bits of hay and dirt dusted its clothes and floated in the ever-growing pool spreading from underneath it. Just like the others, this man was dead and my task was done.

It is time to leave, please. The scared little voice was barely a whisper in the back of my mind, pushing past the thunder of rainwater on the stable's thatched roof.

"If you weren't so eager to run," I replied to the darkness, "we would have time to hide the body... maybe catch another."

I could feel her shrink back at my words and a smile curled my lips.

You promised... Despite the fear I sensed in her, there was also a stubbornness that would stop me if I tried anything beyond what she allowed me.

"Yes," I growled, turning away from the dead man. "How you got that vow from me I still don't understand. But it is not all binding, little one, and I will find a way to break it."

She made no reply.

My clothes soaked through the instant I stepped out of the stables, and the rain washed away the blood from my hands, from my face and neck. But the scarlet stains only seeped into ugly blotches on my skirt and sleeves. The neckline of my hanbok would be ruined. But it didn't matter, because with this death I had drawn one step closer. Closer to fully ridding myself of the girl whose body I had stolen.

A TRAVELER WAS DEAD. Yeona, one of the kitchen girls, found the body not long after sunrise while fetching water from the well. Her screams drew the attention of more than just the village guards, and by the time I reached the stables, a crowd of locals and travelers alike pressed against the perimeter the guardsmen had created around the building.

Seong-Jin let me pass and I went straight over to inspect the corpse. This one was a man; golden hair and light complexion, his clothes suggesting he had come from the northwest. He was face down, which was a relief. If this death was anything like the other half dozen, his wounds weren't something I wanted to see before breakfast. Or after for that matter, or ever again.

The torrential rain from the previous night thickened the scent of horses and hay in the air, the sky was clear morning blue without a trace of clouds, and in no time, it would be safe for the field workers to leave the village and tend the surrounding rice paddies and orchards. I had planned on convincing my father to let me go with, on guard detail or to help the workers. In reality, there was something else I wanted to see. Hidden away in the forest at the foot of our mountain; an old temple.

He must have known that's what I planned and ordered me to investigate the latest death instead. As the magistrate's eldest son, it was part of my duties, but not one I often found more interesting than exploring outside our village's barrier.

I would have come up with some excuse, but his stern look said he still remembered the previous times I'd conveniently made myself scarce to avoid *those* dead bodies.

"His wounds are just like the others." I jumped at Seong-Jin's voice and quickly pulled my thoughts back to the present. "Four marks down the torso, the liver is missing too."

"The only difference is this is a *traveler*," I said. "Not one of the locals."

I looked out of the stable at the crowd and could almost hear the whispers and gossip spreading between mouths. By the time news of this murder got all the way around the village, it would be a twisted variation of the truth. Not that anyone really knew what the truth was in the first place.

"Cover the body," I motioned to another guard standing a few feet away. "Have it brought to Seoyun for further examination."

The man glanced at Seong-Jin, who nodded, before he obeyed. It would be a lie to say I wanted to be head of our village guard – that would keep me here in the same valley, and everyone knew how much more reliable Seong-Jin was than me. But still, the inkling of annoyance persisted whenever they looked to him instead.

You can't have both, Jun. I chided myself. *Let them look to him so you can leave.*

We left the stable and Seong-Jin headed toward the village square; a proper report had to be made and posted. No doubt he expected me to follow, but my attention caught on one particular face in the crowd. She stood at the edge, peering into the stableyard with wide eyes and a furrow in her brow. I switched directions and made my way to her instead. The townsfolk stepped aside for me, but the nosy travelers were slower to move, and I could hear them whispering a little too loud.

"There's a monster on the loose…"

"Thought this was the safest crossing point."

"Targeting foreigners…"

My hand came to rest on the hilt of my sword as I tried to keep it from jostling into anyone, but the motion quieted the voices and gave me more room. My father would be able to handle the unrest; it was nothing I needed to deal with.

Minji didn't take her eyes from the dead body as it was being loaded onto a cart. I came to stand in front of her, blocking her view.

"Minji, what are you doing here?" A flicker of something crossed her face, but it was gone in an instant; just the sun flashing in her dark eyes.

"I was curious," she said, finally meeting my gaze. My little sister, who had nursed an injured magpie back to health, who used to cry so much that our mother didn't make her pluck the dead chickens anymore. She was curious about a dead man?

"It's nothing you want to see, come on." I felt only a brief pang of guilt at abandoning my duty but led the way back out of the yard. *Father just said to go look at it,* I reasoned. *Seong-Jin can handle the report.*

My sister hesitated, casting one last look at the covered cart as it was wheeled off to the healer's, before following me. She slipped her arm through mine as we walked, and a little of the heaviness lifted from my mind.

The village of Dragon River woke earlier than usual; the streets were already filled with a mingle of both foreign and local merchants, on their way to or from some grand, far-off city. The few shops that provided travel necessities were rushing to open and field hands were milling about in search of a morning meal at the community house's kitchen. Word of another murder would soon spoil the familiar atmosphere; already an undercurrent of unease tinged the air.

Our house sat in a small grove of trees down a short alley, and unlike most of the buildings with their thatched roofs, ours had red clay tiles. My mother had recently had the wooden roof beams painted yellow and blue.

"Why did the monster kill a traveler?" Minji asked. We sat on the porch, taking off our shoes before entering the house, and I started at her question. My mind already moving on from that unpleasantness.

"Um...well... We don't know for sure it's a monster." I struggled to think of an answer that would put her at ease. I knew that's what our father suspected and with each new death, that seemed the most likely conclusion. But what kind of monster no one could agree on; a tiger, or a gwishin from deeper in the valley. Or a malevolent forest spirit that somehow made it through both protective walls around the village. But the walls had been created using the magic that flowed through Dragon River and were stronger than most small villages were able to build. It seemed impossible something could have gotten in on its own.

"These aren't normal deaths." Her voice was a whisper, and I was reminded of the winter nights we used to listen to the healer's stories. But we were both older now, and she couldn't hide behind our mother anymore.

No, they were not normal deaths; no human could have caused the kind of wound that had killed those people.

"I heard father say it ate their livers."

"Ji, nothing got past the barriers." I reached over and rested a hand on her head. Her fingers clutched at the fabric of her hanbok, the same color as the sky, and she turned to stare at me. There wasn't any fear in her eyes, just curiosity and almost annoyance.

"Maybe--" She stood abruptly and walked into the house without another word. I stared after her as she disappeared, the sunlight glinting orange on her dark braid.

I was left with an unsettling feeling in my chest, the grove too quiet as though all the birds held their breath. My pulse raced for several beats and I sat on the front steps, trying to banish the look on my sister's face when she had seen the dead traveler. The sense that something wasn't right which had been nagging me all week.

Everything is fine, I told myself, *Minji is fine.* Even if she had been acting strange since the first death.

I followed her in for breakfast.

We had barely sat down at the low table when my father stormed into the main living area.

"Minjun." He loomed above me. "The whole town has gotten it into their heads a goblin broke past the barrier."

"The dokkaebi in this region aren't that dangerous." That was something everyone agreed on, at least among my father's guard. I could tell he was about to send me off on some errand, which meant I would have to wait even longer to get back to the forest temple.

"Seoyun has news and you are coming with me to hear it."

"But Ji and I were—" He cut me off before I could finish coming up with an excuse.

"Your sister will not cover for your slacking this time."

I shot a look at her across the table and she offered an apologetic smile. My mother frowned.

"This is very serious, Jun." She sounded more worried than my father.

I nodded in defeat. The forest would have to wait.

The healer's hut wasn't actually a hut. It was the second-largest building in the village, after the community lodge house. Seoyun was an old woman who had been the doctor for as long as I could remember, and she also served as the village's expert in things beyond the human realm. Like monsters and spirits, and gods who lived inside of the mountains. Her stories filled my childhood.

"You will not like what I have to say." She didn't wait for either of us to fully enter the clinic office before speaking.

The space was small and cluttered with cabinets and shelves loaded to overflowing with parchment and scrolls, precious books stacked on the low table that served as a desk. She wore an apron over her hanbok, and blood splattered the front of it, her sleeves rolled up.

My father sighed like he knew what was coming. I offered a respectful bow when she glanced in my direction and her demeanor changed for an instant as she smiled at me, but the familiar look quickly vanished.

"You can't keep ignoring the truth, Dae-Jung." Seoyun faced him with a tiger glare.

"I had my men check every inch of the outer barrier," he argued. "There wasn't so much as a crack that a spirit could slip through."

I remained silent and listened. So, it was a spirit of some kind doing the killing, which would explain why it was hard to catch.

"This spirit may not have needed a crack in the wall." The old woman held up a small pouch, tipping the contents onto her desk. The morning light that came through the open window landed on a tuft of orange fur; blood matted one end. "A Gumiho is known to take the shape of whoever's heart it eats."

I instantly became alert. A *fox* spirit?

"I didn't think those came up here," I said, reminding them of my presence.

"It is rare, especially for one powerful enough to shapeshift, but not unheard of." My father waved an annoyed hand; he must have heard the intrigue in my voice.

"Based on the bodies, that is my conclusion." Seoyun gripped the bag tightly as she spoke.

"It could be anyone then…" my father muttered.

Anyone… The idea sent a shiver down my spine, but it wasn't entirely fear. It could be one of the field hands who were daily outside the safety of the barrier, or one of the guards who watched for bandits and wild animals. A traveler could have been caught unawares on the road before entering the village.

"Do you know how to stop one?" I tried to recall but she hadn't told many tales about Gumiho.

Seoyun shook her head. "A spirit that strong is beyond my simple knowledge. I was just a girl the last time something like that attacked the village. A monk would know more than me."

My father paced back and forth, his fingers pulling at his beard as he thought. Streaks of grey had started to color his black hair, and I was sure recent events would only add more.

"Minjun." I glanced up from the tuft of fox fur to my father. "All of the creature's victims have been found near the stables. You will set up a watch there tonight."

"What?!" The word was out before I could stop myself, and both Seoyun and my father stared at me. As much as the old stories interested me, the last place I wanted to be was where a Gumiho might be lurking. And it would mean staying up all night. Being too tired in the morning.

"You will watch the stables and tell us who the Gumiho has been masquerading as." He drew out the sentence, enunciating every word to make clear there would be no arguing.

"Alone?" There was a small thread of hope which wilted at the stern expression on his face.

"I have Seong-Jin and the other men already working to keep peace and recheck the barrier's energy, since you were absent while the jobs were being assigned, and in light of the new information, this is your task."

I gripped the hilt of my sword and bowed to hide the look of rebellion I knew he'd see in my eyes.

"Yes, Appa."

Night came all too soon for my liking, clouds scuttling in again from the mountains, heavy with rain, to wash the lands. Minji managed to steal a few rice rolls for me before my father's stare sent me off to the stables, sword at my side and a small lantern in my free hand.

The stables were at the edge of town, up against the inner wall. They housed horses the travelers could rent for their caravans inland. Horses from outside tended to spook too easily at the shadows and whispers that lived in the forests and mountains of our land.

The animals nickered softly when I entered, and a few lifted curious heads as I passed by their stalls, smelling my evening meal. Up in the loft, hay had been piled, easy to toss to the feed troughs and perfect for hiding.

"This is ridiculous," I muttered, settling into the hay and pulling out one of the rice rolls. It was more just to hear something other than the horses and my own breathing, but it *was* unfair to send me alone. I mulled over all the ways I could have avoided it; gone to give the report with Seong-Jin, packed my breakfast and slipped out of the village with the workers. Just refused when my father told me to spy on a fox spirit. Not that any of them would have done me much good.

By the time the intermittent moonlight slanted through the doorway and splashed its silver glow across the packed dirt floor, I had finished my small dinner, dousing my lantern light, and fought the sleep that tried to creep in with it. The rain had yet to come, but the air was heavy with humidity in anticipation, and my hair stuck to the back of my neck.

The faint sound of footsteps broke away from the regular night noises and entered the stables. With some difficulty, I roused myself enough to peer cautiously over the edge of the loft, stifling a yawn.

It was a man; his clothes were dark and close-fitting, and though his hair was black like many of the local folk, his demeanor was distinctly that of a traveler. My father had said nothing about confronting the Gumiho and I had no intention of going beyond what was instructed. I remained hidden and watched.

The man hesitated inside the double doors. He lifted a lantern to scan his surroundings and the light illuminated his confused expression. He called quietly into the far corners of the stable, but no reply answered.

Why would he risk setting up a meeting here after dark with all the murders?

Another figure stood in the doorway, appearing as though from the darkness. I hadn't even heard their approach like I had the traveler. It was a woman; the silver light at her back cast her face into shadow and picked out the fluttering strands of her dark hair, which had come loose from its braid.

She wore a hanbok; the skirt hiked up to her knees and tied with a sash for easier movement. A small nagging feeling in the back of my mind whispered I should recognize her.

The man turned quickly and thrust his lantern out. The yellow light swung wildly across the woman's face, and I barely managed to keep from cursing aloud.

"The village is not safe to wander alone, traveler." Minji did not blink, and the look from before was in her eyes again, glowing red in the firelight. I stared at the two, the truth trying to force its way to the front of my mind, but I refused to let it. *It is not her. Not my little sister.*

"I could say the same to you, little girl." The man affected an air of confidence, but there was an edge to his tone that suggested otherwise. "Perhaps we should both head back to someplace safe."

Anger prickled under my skin at the suggestion and I almost stepped out from my hiding spot. Gumiho or not, if he laid a finger on my sister, he would find himself in need of a new hand. Minji's voice stopped me halfway from standing.

"I did not come out to be safe, little boy." A smile spread too wide across her face and curled back her lips. Sharp teeth glinted in the lantern light and she was suddenly not my sister anymore; she was a monster. The air rippled around her, nine ghostly fox tails rustling the fabric of her hanbok as they became more solid and swept across the ground behind her, and the truth became real with them.

I didn't see her move; the traveler's lantern hit the dirt floor and shattered open, dashing the flame. Lighting streaked across the sky and the following clap of thunder drowned out the sound of him dying.

The horses kicked up a fuss, whinnying loudly and stamping the ground in fright. I threw myself back into the haystack, unable to watch the thing that had been my sister. The rice cakes threatened to force their way back up my throat, and I bit down on the inside of my cheek till I tasted blood. The rain finally released from the clouds and thundered against the world; my head resounded with the echo.

No, no no... Not Minji, please. How could it be her? Out of everyone why was it *her*? When had she ever been outside the village alone? Except...the day I found the temple at the foot of the mountains, inside the forest. We had been out collecting wild herbs as a surprise gift for our mother. I found an overgrown trail, but she hadn't wanted to follow it. So, I told her to wait in sight of the rice paddy guards and went off to investigate. I couldn't have been gone more than five minutes and she was sitting sulkily by a tree when I came back. She looked no different, but...it had happened exactly a week ago, and that night the first body had been found.

I had let the fox spirit into the village. And it was my sister.

Soon all I could hear was the monsoon and the howling of the wind.

———

IT WAS RAINING AGAIN, as if the gods knew how much I hated getting soaked through. The trees outside her house provided little protection from the torrential downpour but I stopped under their branches to be sure all of the blood had washed off this time.

"You've been unusually quiet tonight, little one."

I have nothing to say.

I paused by the back door, a shiver racing down my spine. She always had something to say after a kill; begging, pleading despite our bargain. My ears strained for danger as my entire body became alert. "What have you done?"

No reply, but I could feel her secrets hidden just outside of my reach.

"What happened during the day that you're not telling me about?!"

Nothing...little fox.

Rainwater coursed down my face and into my mouth, but I couldn't move, eyes darting from shadow to shadow and seeing only imaginary shapes in the dark. I would not be bested by a mortal girl; she would not be the one to steal my freedom.

Finally, I crept back into the house and changed out of my soaked clothes. Neither of her parents stirred when I snuck past their room, and a new thought occurred to me.

"Secrets are dangerous," I whispered. "And I am very good at learning them."

THE SOUND of shouting voices broke through the fog in my mind. Hay stabbed through my clothes, and slowly the night's events resurfaced, forcing me awake.

"How are you going to protect us?" I didn't recognize the voice. Warily I peered over the edge of the loft and down at the huddle of men below. My father and Seong-Jin stood over the dead traveler, and in the morning sun, I could see now that the man had been much older than I thought.

"We are working to apprehend the murderer—" My father spoke to a different traveler who stood just inside the stable doors.

"For a whole week you've been saying that and now whatever it is has started to kill us!" the man's voice rose to a near shout. I could hear the sounds of another crowd gathered outside and, by the hard look on my father's face, knew the situation was quickly spiraling out of control.

I should go down, I thought, *tell them what I saw.* But it was Minji, my *sister* I had seen.

"We have a promising lead—" Seong-Jin tried to speak now, but the traveler interrupted him as well.

"Promising lead?!" he demanded. "Any number of cursed monsters could be in this village."

Seong-Jin glowered but said nothing. He would make a better son for my father.

I felt sick to my stomach and pressed back against the hay, focusing on drawing in enough air. *Come on, Minjun, you have to go down there and tell them. At least tell Appa.*

I barely heard what was being said, my heart loud as last night's storm in my ears as I scrambled to the ladder and then the stable floor. A heavy hand clamped shut on my shoulder even before I realized I had been heading for the door. This would be so much easier if I didn't have to look at the man my sister had killed while telling my father she was the one who'd done it.

"Minjun."

He was very angry.

"Yes…" I lifted my head and met his gaze. I could see

Seong-Jin and the other traveler in my peripheral vision but didn't dare look away from my father.

"Our promising lead…?" He prompted through gritted teeth.

"I'd rather tell you in private." *At least send the traveler away.* He didn't need to know about how terribly I'd messed up.

"The people have a right to know what is going on," the man huffed. "Six have died already."

"Father, please." My voice wavered and he sighed. I could see it in his gaze; he thought I had fallen asleep and had nothing to report.

"Seong-Jin, please step outside with Mr. Zander. I will speak with my son in private."

Seong-Jin bowed and moved to guide the angry traveler out of the stables. The man resisted only a little but eventually let himself be ushered into the crowd, no doubt to incite even more unrest. My father turned back to face me.

"Well?"

"I saw the Gumiho."

Silence met my statement, then… "You swear it?"

I swallowed hard and nodded. "Yes, on my ancestors, I saw who killed this man. And all the others."

He was quiet again and waited for me to explain. Was I meant to say it just like that?

"It was…Minji. I…I saw her kill the traveler." The image rose too vivid in my mind. "She tore out his liver… I think she ate it."

Pain exploded across my face, and a moment later, I was staring at the dirt floor on my knees, my hand inches away from a splotch of partially dried blood. My cheek throbbed from where my father had struck me and I stumbled back to my feet, head spinning.

"Why…?"

"How *dare* you." There was no mistaking the rage in his voice. "You would accuse your own *sister* of being possessed by a monster before admitting to failure? After every time she has covered your laziness, your irresponsibility and selfishness."

I stared at him.

"I am telling the truth," I insisted. "Why would I make that up? If all you expected of me was to fail, why give me the task in the first place?"

My father's gaze burned into me and the last tethers of fatigue and stress strained in that look.

"I swear it," I said again, surprised by the angry tears that clouded my vision.

"Impossible."

"Father—"

"Silence!" His voice slammed against me harder than his hand had and the words choked inside of me. Shuffling footsteps at the stable door announced Seong-Jin's return. He looked between me and my father, an uncertain question on his face.

Maybe he would believe me…

"Take my son to the guardhouse and lock him up." I spun back around and gaped at my father.

"What?!"

Seong-Jin hesitated, just as surprised as I was at my father's order.

"I do not have time for your incompetence. You will

stay there until I can deal with you properly." He glared at Seong-Jin to comply and the other boy bowed.

"Please, you have to believe me." My hand went to the hilt of my sword before I realized I'd left it up in the loft. "There might be a way to save her."

There had to be a way to save her.

My father turned his back and stared down at the dead traveler. Panic started to claw its way up my throat, and I stepped away from Seong-Jin when he approached.

"Come on, Jun." He sounded sympathetic and I scowled. "I'm sorry."

He really was the son my father wanted. And I was the one who let my sister's heart be eaten by a Gumiho.

I bolted out into the stableyard. The gathered crowd pressed against the guards trying to hold a perimeter, and Seong-Jin called after me, the shouts drawing the attention of his men. My men technically, not that I wanted them to be. One stepped into my path as I tried to escape into the bustle of people and grabbed my arm, wrenching me to a halt. I spun with the force and slammed my fist into his nose. He stumbled backward with a cry, and red ran down his face; the townsfolk closest scrambled back in alarm.

"Stop him!"

I wasn't sure who shouted, Seong-Jin or my father, but I pushed into the crowd as the other guards rushed to obey. I didn't know what I was going to do if I got away, but if I was locked up then there would be nothing I *could* do.

Someone shoved me from the right and I stumbled to regain my balance. Another blow hit my shins, and I just managed to catch myself. I barely made it out of the stable-yard when the traveler from before struck and sent me to the ground. Pain shot through my palms as I tried to keep my head from slamming against the dirt road, and a second later the man's foot collided with my stomach. I tumbled a few feet, vision blurred as another blow hit too near my face. More of them appeared and they pressed in on my prone form and began to beat me. I struggled to cover my head and curled around my middle; I could taste blood in my mouth. It was like they had been waiting to unleash their pent-up fear and I had just given them a perfect excuse.

"That's enough!" This was my father, and what felt like an eternity later, the blows ceased. My ears were ringing and I was hauled painfully to my feet. They had at least bruised several ribs, if not broken them, and after my vision stopped swirling, I stared into the face of my father.

"The prison, Seong-Jin." I didn't fight this time.

The prison cells were just a row of barred huts behind the guardhouse. Open to the elements but the door faced the tall stone wall of the inner barrier. Yeona was sent to make sure my injuries weren't too serious, but it was obvious she had been told not to talk to me. Her gaze remained downcast, focused on bandaging my hands where the skin had been torn in my attempt to protect my face, and despite multiple questions, she refused to respond. Once again, I was left by myself.

I paced the small space, my mind a chaos of thoughts. The truth sunk its claws into my heart, sending a chill over my whole body. I had let the Gumiho take her. I didn't even *notice* for a whole week what had happened. Too busy dreaming of the temple, of the things I might find inside its ruins if I could just get away long enough to explore.

"Your father told me what you said."

I turned toward Seong-Jin. He stood just outside my cell, arms crossed and leaning against the stone wall.

"You have to believe I'm telling the truth."

"Really? Because she is the last person who could be a Gumiho."

"Which is why you know I'm not lying." I gripped the iron bars of my cell. "Please, you have to let me out."

He shook his head and rubbed a hand along his chin. The motion was startlingly similar to my father, and I tried to ignore the twinge of jealousy.

"Master Choi doesn't even believe you, and you're his son." He met my gaze and held it. "This is bad even for you, Jun."

Heat rose to my face, but could I really blame him for not believing me? It wouldn't be the first time I'd modified the truth to avoid trouble.

"I saw her."

He shook his head again and pushed from the wall. There was a brief look of doubt that crossed his face, but it fled too quickly. He wouldn't disobey my father, especially not for me.

Someone must have appeared at the end of the row of cells because he bowed suddenly.

"Mrs. Choi."

My mother stopped in front of him.

"Lee Seong-Jin, my husband is looking for you." Her face held the same worry I had seen yesterday morning. Seong-Jin bowed again, and with one last glance in my direction, he marched off.

"Minjun." The frown fully clouded my mother's expression, her eyes watery when she peered up at me. "Tell me what happened."

I stared down at my bandaged hands on the iron bars.

"She killed the traveler."

"I have seen how my daughter was acting different and now I know why, but I want you to tell me *how it happened*." What I heard in her quiet voice was somehow worse than all of my father's rage.

"I...left her alone, by the forest edge," I rushed to explain everything. "There was an old temple I found and wanted to explore but she...she didn't, so I told her to wait. I was only gone..."

Five minutes, I wasn't gone for that long... The memory of her unhappy frown and the way she complained at being left alone resurfaced, and I knew that I had been gone longer than five minutes. If it hadn't been for her coming along to the forest, I would have had time to explore more, and I'd been reluctant to return to where I had left her.

"I was gone for too long," I said, resting my forehead against the bars of my cell.

"Jun," my mother's hands wrapped around mine, warm and calloused, "I have known since you were young that you never wanted this to be your home forever. But us, your family, that responsibility does not change no matter where you call home."

I didn't want her to be right, but my head refused to let my wandering heart win this battle. I knew she was right, and I had neglected more than just my duties to the village by letting my desires blindly drive me.

She reached into the pouch at her waist and withdrew a

ring of keys. "I cannot change anyone else's mind. They don't love her like I do, which means you are the only one who can save your sister."

"But how am I..." I stared at the keys which she had obviously stolen from my father and tried to think of an excuse. She paused and looked at me expectantly.

No more excuses.

"I need to find a monk," I said instead. Seoyun had mentioned in her office they would know more about powerful spirits.

She nodded once and unlocked my cell. "There won't be any in this region. They stay near the larger towns and cities."

The nearest town was three days away. That meant three more nights my sister would kill, three more deaths in our little village. Not to mention the time it would take to get back. There was no way my father could keep order for that long, but I didn't have any other options.

"I'm sorry." My voice came out a whisper and she pulled me into a tight embrace.

"I know, darling, I know."

She stepped back. "Go, there is a pack at the base of the cherry tree with all you will need. And take this."

The pendant she handed me was carved from jade, the snarling face of a dragon glaring up at me. It was a safety charm, a little piece of the same magic that protected our village and the symbol of my family.

No more excuses.

The air was heavy with humidity and dread. Darkness had yet to fall completely, but the workers were inside already. I snuck my way back to the stables by the inner gate, taking a more roundabout route to collect the pack my mother had hidden. Thankfully, my sword was also still nestled into the hay where I'd left it, and I strapped it to my belt. Now to just get past the guards. The ones by the outer barrier wall would be trickier to avoid.

The two men at the inner gate were talking quietly to each other about the weather. It seemed neither wanted to think on the terrible week, and I couldn't blame them. I didn't want to think about all the deaths either, but now there was no avoiding it. Not if I wanted to fix my mistake.

"Good evening." All three of us turned at the greeting. It was Minji.

What is she doing here? It was barely sunset and there were still people milling within sight; she couldn't possibly be here to kill these men…right?

The guards recovered themselves and bowed, only a shallow bob of the head, and smiled.

"Mother said I should bring something to drink." She held a pitcher in one hand and a stack of cups in the other. The men murmured their thanks as she filled each of them a cup. "There's enough for the others too," she added. One of the guards turned to call over the short distance to where two men stood at the outer gate.

Father would be furious if he saw how they left their post and came to stand with the others around my sister, her smile inviting. I sent a prayer of thanks to my mother and darted past the inner wall and across the short distance to the shadow of the barrier gatehouse. The hair on the back of my neck tingled and I shot a glance over my shoulder, hand gripping the gate ring.

Minji stared directly at me, her expression almost

blank. The fading light looked orange in her hair again, and even across the grassy expanse that separated the walls, I could see a flash of red in her dark eyes. My feet felt frozen to the ground and I couldn't make myself look away from her terrible gaze. If I turned my back, she would tear out my heart in seconds.

"I'll save you this time, Minji," I whispered. "I promise."

For a moment, the foxlike look was gone from her face and my sister stared back at me. A ghost smile touched her lips and she nodded. She knew that I had seen her the other night, and she was distracting the guards so I could get out. A small hope burned in my chest; if she was still in there, then there had to be a way to get the Gumiho out.

I spun around and shoved the gate wide enough to slip through and stole out into the twilight, beyond the safety of the village, beyond the barrier that kept out the monsters and spirits that roamed the night.

I COULDN'T BELIEVE *she had tricked me. Anger coursed like fire through my veins as I stormed back through the streets of the village. It would have been perfect if the stupid girl hadn't ruined our bargain and let her brother slip away to get help.*

You aren't the only clever one, Gumiho. *She sounded insufferably smug.*

"But you are the only one who has something to lose, little one," *I growled.* "You have betrayed me."

I was never trying to help you.

This was why the others warned against bargains, letting humans willingly give their hearts to be eaten instead of just taking it by force. I should have known better than to accept her terms, but the prospect of an entire village, unaware of my hungry presence till it was too late, had been too tempting and her such a soft creature.

And I would have her body, unmarred by my killing touch, after they were all dead.

The girl's house came into view, shrouded in shadows, and smoke from the kitchen curled up into the late lavender sky. It was going to rain again; I could smell it on the breeze and it mingled with the scent of human warmth. My senses heightened as night ambled in and my mind narrowed to its task.

What are you doing? *Fear crept into her whisper, and a grin stretched across my face. The floor groaned under my feet as I made my way toward the kitchen, not bothering to remove my dusty shoes. I would take advantage of her brother's absence, the only human who knew the truth. And I would start with her family.*

―――

THE ROAD to the nearest large town ran almost parallel to Dragon River, the namesake of our village. Bridges had been built across a few of the narrower sections in order to reach the rice paddies nestled up the foot of our mountain. The rain-swelled water drowned out the sound of my pounding feet; I didn't stop running till my side felt like a dagger had been wedged beneath my ribcage. The village was only a cluster of lantern light in the darkness now and I couldn't tell how far I'd actually gone. I wasn't going to be fast enough on foot. Why hadn't I taken one of the horses?

It's not like I can get in even more trouble. Three days was an eternity away; the whole village could be dead by the time I got there and back again with a monk.

My mother's words from before pushed me on as clouds rolled in to hide the rising moon, and I rummaged frantically through my pack. There was money and some food and I was relieved to find a small lantern with some oil.

Living inside the safety of our village, it was easy to forget the real dangers the elders warned us about. Goblins, wicked spirits, gods who were the very heart of mountains... Since I was young, I dreamed of leaving the village and going out to explore. Find all the terrifying and fantastical creatures Seoyun told us about, my sister and me. While she would hide her face in our mother's skirts, I leaned toward the stories and tried to memorize their shapes, the way they sounded in the glowing light of the lanterns. I wanted to see those places.

Minji's wicked grin right before she killed the traveler flashed through my mind. I gripped the hilt of my sword and pressed forward, the light from my lantern barely illuminating the ground at my feet. It was very different to fight a monster when it was someone you loved, and you were the reason they were no longer human.

A heavy drop of water hit the top of my head and slid down beneath the collar of my shirt. A second later, the rain fell from the clouds like an overturned bucket. I quickly tried to shelter my feeble light and cursed my haste and stupidity. Of course, it was going to rain; all the other nights it had and monsoon season was fully upon us.

Now it really was impossible to see, and if I stayed out on the open road, I would end up in the river. I stumbled across one of the bridges and scampered up into the relative safety of the forest. There was a small hut used to store old farm equipment somewhere, and it would be a better alternative to huddling under a tree. I pushed into the soaked underbrush, floundering as thorns and branches tried to catch my legs and clothes.

This is ridiculous. My sister is counting on me this time and I can't even leave sight of home without getting into trouble. My clothes were heavy with water, and the rain sliding from summer leaves slicked hair to my face no matter how many times I brushed it out of the way. The sleeve of my jacket caught on a branch and pulled me off balance. The lantern slipped from my grasp and the light was lost to the forest. Or to something else; a devious chuckle echoed from the dark, bouncing between the trees so that I couldn't pinpoint the source.

I yanked my sword free from its scabbard, dropping the sheath in the process, and forced my way through the dark. *Just get back to the road.* The forest had been a bad idea; those seemed to be the only kind I could have. I stumbled into a clearing and it took me a second to realize I could see. An iron lantern swung sharply above an old archway covered in moss and climbing plants. The ancient temple. I had somehow found myself back where it had all gone wrong in the first place.

I cautiously approached the open entrance, wooden doors rotted to almost nothing, and peered into the courtyard. It was dimly lit by another two lanterns near one of the side buildings. If this temple was set up similar to the one in the village, then it was probably a storage shed. The main sanctuary was only a looming shadow farther back;

the lantern light glinting off rain-soaked stone and wet metal hinges that flashed like eyes in the dark. When lightning briefly illuminated the world, I could see its caved-in roof.

I could go back to the road and keep heading to the large town. Maybe avoid another Gumiho or some other dreadful creature hiding here. Lightning cut through the sky again, followed swiftly by a deafening crack of thunder; the ground vibrated with the sound. It wouldn't do any good to continue on in the storm.

Mysterious temple dweller it is.

I kept my sword at the ready and tried the handle of the shed door; it pushed inward with little resistance, and inside a fire burned in a dirt pit lined with stones. Dust-covered pots, mostly scattered and broken, occupied the storage room. A few rotten wood shelves lined the walls.

"Hello?" I stepped out of the rain. Shadows moved near the back corner and a man straightened up.

"Traveler? Wanderer?" His voice was scratchy and low, and when he turned, lightning pale eyes sent a shiver down my spine. "Villager."

"May I take shelter here?" Even as the words left my mouth, I hoped he'd say no.

"Of course." He smiled and it was surprisingly gentle. "Thank you for asking."

I swallowed my fear and shuffled over to the fire. The man ambled to place a small handful of sticks into the flames and then slowly lowered himself to sit. Deep lines creased his angular face and his gnarled hair had twigs and leaves stuck in it.

"Thank you, grandfather." The silence was nearly unbearable. He looked up and smiled again.

"You are looking for something, young man."

I stared at him.

"Why else would you be out in such a storm, alone and scared?"

"I'm on my way to the next town over." I glanced back to the door.

"Ah, it must be important."

"I…yes, it is."

The man nodded as though he weren't surprised in the least. I shifted uncomfortably in my wet clothes; the fire slowly dried them.

"It must have something to do with magic too."

My eyes widened and a knowing look stole across his face. *How does he…*

"Are you a monk?" I blurted out. He laughed, though it sounded more like an earthquake.

"No, but I know quite a lot about this mountain and the spirits who dwell in and around it."

"You know about the Gumiho?" If he could help me, then I wouldn't have to walk all the way to the next town.

"Yes," he said, cautiously. "I know about Gumiho. Dangerous spirits."

"Please, I need to know how to get rid of one without harming the person whose body it stole."

It was his turn to look surprised.

"Save the Gumiho?"

"No. Save the person who the Gumiho is possessing. Is there a way?" *Please, please, please.*

The man tugged thoughtfully on his long scraggly

beard and muttered to himself. "Very difficult…better to kill it."

"It's my sister." The confession burned in my chest, and the rest of it wouldn't come out. "I know she's still in there, I can see it in her eyes when she is herself and not the fox."

"Yes, sometimes that can happen, but it will not last for long."

"Then help me, please."

"Mistakes like this are not so easily fixed." The old man's tone suggested he knew it was my fault, even without asking. "The easy route is to kill the Gumiho instead, drown it. But if you think it isn't too late…"

He motioned to a dusty, half-rotten shelf. "Take one of those."

I stood and pushed aside the leaves growing through a crack in the wall. Among the shards of broken clay, one pot remained intact.

"That will trap the fox spirit, and after one hundred days, your sister will be released from its hold."

I lifted the dark clay pot; it was nearly as large as my torso but lighter than it looked. How was I meant to use this to trap her? Should I even risk trying it and still needing to go find a proper monk?

"All you must do is remove the lid when she is next to it."

"Thank you." I turned and bowed, pressing my forehead to the ground. This man certainly held knowledge of spirits, if he wasn't one himself; his strangely pale eyes saw more than was visible. I had to take the risk. "I'll give you whatever you want—"

"Do not thank me with words," the man interrupted,

and I lifted my head. "Whether you save her or not, you must return here. Then I will accept your true thanks, if you still want to give it."

I opened my mouth, but he raised a silencing hand.

"I don't expect one as young as you to remember how this mountain used to be," he croaked. "Go, when the rain stops, and hope it is not too late."

Thunder shook the temple stones again, and somewhere outside of our little shelter, lightning struck a tree, sending it crashing to the forest floor. I jumped at the sound and spun toward the door; laughter crept beneath the wooden slats.

"How—" When I turned back around, the old man was gone.

For a long while, I sat by the fire and dried my clothes. The monsoon raged outside and I pretended not to notice the creatures that prowled the temple with glinting eyes as they peered through cracks in the door. They were probably just dokkaebi goblins which would normally be no trouble to deal with. That is, if I weren't alone. But whatever monsters they were, none tried to get into the little storage building, and despite my best efforts, sleep clouded my exhausted mind.

I woke with a start and opened my eyes to a single ray of morning sunlight directly on my face. The rain had stopped and sounds of the waking forest could be heard again. I thought briefly of searching for the old man, but his warning left a sliver of doubt in my mind. The contents of my pack were soaked and I left them by the burned-down firepit by way of thanks instead, if he was a spirit. The Onggi pot just barely fit in their place. Using the roar of Dragon River as my guide, I left the old temple ruins and forged my way back to the main road.

The village was at the beginning of a valley. Two mountains stretched out like raised arms from it, and in the already warm summer morning, green covered them like silken cloth. Breaking from the trees, I could see the village just across the river. I had made it farther than I realized last night. The slope of rice paddies provided an elevated view and the miniature streets appeared deserted; a single curl of smoke rose from where my house was hidden in its small grove of ginkgo trees.

The closer I came to the outer barrier, the more the silence grew. No one worked the paddies or orchards near the wall, and the normal bustle of travelers coming and going on the main road was absent. The front gate was shut fast, and dread writhed in my stomach.

I wasn't gone more than a few hours; everything couldn't have gone wrong that quickly. I knocked on the gate, but no answering call came. The pot had grown heavy from the walk down the mountain, and I slipped the pack from my shoulders, setting it against the stone gate post.

"Hello?!" It was locked from the outside; I yanked the wooden beam from where it blocked the gate, and I peered into the grassy area beyond. The yard between the barrier and the inner wall was deserted. No guards at either post and the streets were even emptier than they had looked from the forest. I kept my sword at the ready as I moved slowly into the village.

The grass was torn up in places by hooves, and a quick glance into the stableyard revealed the doors thrown open and no sounds from within. All the horses were gone.

It took me the whole way up to the community house to notice the smell. The recent rain masked it well, but there was no mistaking the scent of fresh blood. And now I noticed the broken windows, doors torn apart, and dark stains on the wooden boards of the community house porch. But still no sign of the people, alive or dead. *Where is everyone?*

My quick breathing was the loudest sound in the village and I faltered in the middle of the road. *I should check inside the community house,* I thought, though my legs refused to move.

"Minjun!" I spun at the sound of my sister's voice and narrowly avoided impaling her on the end of my sword. She stopped short and clasped a hand over her mouth.

"Ji?" I lowered the blade so it didn't point directly at her but kept it ready. I couldn't help the small flare of relief at the sight of her.

"I'm so glad you came back." She lifted her gaze and smiled. A little too wide.

"Where is everyone? Where are mother and father?"

"After you left, a traveler broke into our house. Father is dead."

My heart stopped, but she kept talking.

"Then when Seong-Jin tried to punish him, everyone turned on each other, and he died too. It was chaos, all those people so full of fear and no one to aim it at but each other. Most ran away, but not all escaped."

This was not my sister. Too clever eyes watched me intently as I tried to circle around toward the gates, but she kept moving to block my path.

Why'd you leave the pot at the gate?! I forced down my

panic, the sick feeling in my stomach, and asked, "Can you show me? I would like to see them."

"Of course. I left them at the house." She took a few steps and waited to see if I'd follow before leading the way down the side alley. She glanced back often and I tried to see past the Gumiho, searching desperately for any trace of the real Minji.

Blood smeared the floor of the main room inside our house. It was no more than a day old, and I stepped to avoid it.

"See, the wicked foreigners killed them." She motioned into the sectioned-off area that was our parent's bedroom, and in the dim light that fell through the open door, I could see two bodies lying on the mats. My father and...it was Seong-Jin, not my mother. He had died doing what I should have, protecting my family.

I couldn't force myself to check how they had died, but I didn't need to; the blank look on Minji's face as she stared into the room told me everything I needed to know. The old man had been right, mistakes like this were not easily fixed. Especially when the problem started well before the fox spirit.

"Brother?" She stood right next to me and I nearly dropped my sword, scrambling back to put space between us. "I'm so glad you're back."

I needed to get the pot. Grieving would have to wait unless I wanted to join the dead in the afterlife. I didn't think my father could be any less disappointed in me there either, but he would certainly try.

"Do you think you could make me something to eat?"

Her eyes narrowed.

"You're hungry?"

"Yes." I needed to distract her long enough to escape. "I didn't get any supper and it will give me strength to bury them."

I hesitated, then added, "You know it's what we should do."

I offered a sad smile and, with great effort, rested a hand on her head like I used to when we were younger, when she was just an innocent girl and all I could be blamed for was daydreaming too much.

"Of course," she nodded emphatically, eyeing my sword. She started to the kitchen but stopped abruptly and spun back around. "I don't want you running off before you have your meal; can't work on an empty stomach."

She snatched a ball of twine from our mother's sewing basket and quick as a fox had the thread knotted around my ankles before I knew what was going on. She smiled a satisfied sort of smile and, with a knowing look, disappeared around the corner to the kitchen.

I lifted my sword to slice the thread when she gave it a tug to ensure I was still on the other end.

No! My heart lurched as I scanned the room frantically, and my search fell on the low table we used to eat at. The tug came again and I cut the twine a second later, fingers fumbling to tie it around the table leg.

I darted from the house and down the alley back to the main street and glanced around. She had been telling the truth in that regard anyway; the people really had fled. I prayed my mother was one of them. She had known Minji was the Gumiho, and hopefully, that was enough to protect her.

Get to the gate, Jun.

A loud wail shattered the quiet air. I didn't wait for her to appear at the mouth of the alley and took off toward the outer barrier, where I had foolishly left the old man's pot.

"Brother! Come back!"

I didn't glance behind me; I didn't want to see her face or I wouldn't be able to keep running. If the pot failed, then I could seal the gate again and hope it would hold while I found a monk. But it had been made to keep monsters out, not in. I cut through the backyard of a few huts, a quicker route to the main gate, and finally stumbled across some of the people who hadn't made it out. They wore villager garb, but I didn't slow down; I knew I'd recognize their faces if I looked. The path took me past the cells and the stench of blood was almost overpowering. I slipped on the muddy ground as I staggered onto the main road again. From this angle, I could see across the yard into the stable and realized someone had tried to burn it down, the interior charred black and smoldering faintly. I didn't stop to stare for long, bolting through the inner gate. The stables had been the Gumiho's killing ground and they had probably hoped to trap it inside the fire.

A hand grasped the back of my shirt, and a second later, we crashed to the ground. I rolled to keep from landing on my blade and felt teeth or claws tear my shoulder, losing hold of the weapon. She pressed her knees down on my arms, her hands scrambling for my throat. Staring up at her, I could see her hair was streaked with orange, face twisted. Blood stained her sharp teeth and triumph lit black eyes.

The fox spirit made her stronger than normal, but I

managed to grab her wrists and pull her off-balance, shoving all my weight to one side. I staggered back to my feet and, as she struggled to free her legs from the long skirt of her hanbok, dove for my pack.

The strap snapped and the pot tumbled out of the gate, toward the river.

"No!" I shouted. It teetered by the edge and I threw myself at it, feeling the tip of her claws against the back of my neck.

"Come back!" Her growl was barely human, but the words stuck in my chest. They were ones I'd heard my sister say to me many times. I grasped the pot in my arms. Her hands reached for me again but she tripped over my legs in her mad frenzy.

Dragon River roared hungrily, and the waters reached to drag her in. I didn't think – I grabbed her hand with both of mine and refused to let the river have her. For a brief moment, the panic that was on the Gumiho face changed and it was Minji clinging to my arm. It was her, and hope filled her eyes.

I pulled her up from the steep bank and the moment was gone. Pain burst through my chest as the Gumiho desperately tried to take my heart, claws sinking into my skin. The pot lay just within arm's reach.

"I'm sorry, Minji," I wheezed.

She opened her mouth, but I didn't wait for any taunting words. I kept hold of her with one hand and with the other yanked off the pot's lid. Her eyes widened in fear and she tried to pull away.

A black mist spilled from the pot and curled around her body. It was cold, but I didn't let go of her as she began to tremble, and she screamed. Her body shifted; the fox spirit no longer able to hold the illusion of my sister as it shrunk her back to its original form. Dark orange fur streaked with my blood and its nine tails tipped in black.

Minji stopped struggling and lay still.

It can't be too late... I saw her in there. I clung to that thread of hope, more desperate than sure. The Onggi pot no longer looked too small to hold her in this shape. I carefully lifted the fox, feeling her faint heartbeat pulse against my hands, and placed her inside. The dark mist dissipated as I resealed the pot with the lid.

I remained sitting at the river's edge till the sun sank low over the mountains and the waters glittered with the orange light. The wound on my chest was shallow, but pain radiated through my body with even the slightest of movements. It would rain again tonight and I couldn't just sit there and wait for it.

Wearily, I climbed to my feet and looked back at Dragon River village, my home though it had never felt like it till now. Now that I had lost it. I needed to bury my father, and whoever else was still there. I needed to learn what had become of my mother and the others who had fled.

"Forgive me," I whispered to my family, to the whole village. My vision blurred as I retrieved the pack and secured the pot and Gumiho inside. Only one strap was still fully intact, but I would have time to go in search of a new one. The tears were sticky on my face, and I couldn't remember when I had stopped crying.

Come on, Jun, mistakes aren't easily fixed. The old man's words echoed hollowly inside me. I understood what he meant about my true thanks; I didn't want to give it anymore. But I would return to the ancient temple anyways, after the one hundred days, after I made sure Minji would be human again.

Because he had only said it wasn't easy to fix, but not *impossible...*

OF UNDERWOODS AND UNDERWORLDS

BY HANNAH CARTER

"Someone really ought to write an instruction manual for one of these things!" I shrieked as my monstrous creation thundered through the downtown boulevard.

People screamed; innocent vegetables were trampled; a few birds might have dropped some excrement as they flew away. I, on the other hand, clung to the tangible darkness on the beast.

"Someone *did*!" Zelda, my older sister, yelled in my ear. "It's called a *spellbook*, and when I tried to read you the instructions, you said that it was *boring*!"

We collided with a vendor selling home-crafted pots and pans...or, at least, that was what they had *previously* sold. Now they had a very promising future in the busted shards business.

"Sorry!" I yelled over my shoulder before I directed my next response to Zelda. "Well, what I mean by that is— someone ought to make one that doesn't put me to sleep immediately! I have a very short atte—*duck*!"

Zelda shoved me down as we passed under the arm of a statue dedicated to some ugly old dude with a beard.

"Stop this thing, Haddie!" Zelda pounded at the beast, which only roared in response. Flames of darkness shot up from its body and enveloped the world for a few seconds.

"That isn't helping!" I gripped the fur and pulled backward.

"*Nothing* is!" Zelda punched me in the shoulder. "I sure wish someone had thought to write down the step-by-step process on how to properly conjure and control one of these things. Oh, wait! I remember. Do *you* remember what that mystical little book is called?"

"I really don't need your attitude right now!" I elbowed her, but she only tightened her grip on me. That was really for the best, anyway, since the creature leaped over a small waterway and landed on the other side.

"*Girls!*" An explosion of light blanketed the sky as the head prefect of our magic academy appeared right in our path. He held out his hand as white light pierced the dark hide of our monster.

The creature snorted and backed away, but I could feel something brewing inside of it. "Percy, wait just a second if you don't mind—"

"Now's not any time for your shenanigans or stalling, Haddie Underwood." Percy glared at us both. That was the worst thing about Perce, out of the many I had to choose from: he sounded like an old man, despite the fact he'd just had his seventeenth birthday. "You deliberately put the town and Morgana Hall in danger. And as for you, Zelda, as a newly minted prefect, I expected better behavior out of you than to let your younger sister run amuck in town."

Zelda dipped her blonde head and held me closer. "My sister didn't mean any harm. She's—she's—"

"Reckless with magic, a danger to all decent society, a scourge on Morgana Hall, and the blackest name on the ignominious family tree of the Underwood dynasty?"

In retrospect, Percy did two things at that exact moment that sealed his fate.

Mistake one: he lowered his hand, ever so slightly, so that his light was no longer at eye level with my beast.

Mistake two: he also shifted his weight closer to us, probably in hopes of continuing his pompous lecture.

Unfortunately, there would be no time for him to make a mistake three. My monster roared with such ferocity that Zelda and I were almost thrown from his back, but Percy unequivocally had it worse.

The beast lunged at Percy and devoured our head prefect in one gobble.

———

"—A *danger* to society, a scourge—Haddie, are you even listening to me?" Zelda gave me a kick in the back of my leg as we walked along the side of the beast. I stumbled forward and clutched the mane or whatnot of my creature to keep from tripping.

"I am, but it's not like I haven't heard it before. Literally just a few minutes ago right before this—this *thing* polished off Percy!" I gestured to the monster. He huffed and grunted as we traveled up the cliffside path that wound all the way up to Morgana Hall, our lovely torture chamber. Or, as some might refer to it, a magical boarding school. The stone castle, with all its turrets, windows, and secrets—including one semi-dead body of the fabled King Arthur—stood on the top of a seaside precipice. "But at least he seems a bit calmer now. The...the beast thing, not Percy."

"He's probably in a food coma!" Zelda tugged on one of my brown pigtails. "Which, I suppose, bodes well for us. Hopefully we'll have time to get back up to Headmistress Demetria and say, 'Oh, sorry, this thing ate your son,' before the creature devours us."

I giggled. Tall beach grass tickled my legs, and I scratched at the itches as we hiked up the curvy incline. "Oh, don't worry. You know Headmistress Demetria will fix everything with a wave of her hand. And even if she's mad, all she'll probably do is just turn us into frogs or something like that for a few hours, tops."

"Haddie," Zelda sighed. "Can't you ever take your studies seriously? As secondborn of the Underwood girls, you'll be called off to do fantastic things one day. You could scour the deserts of Aurabia for hidden jewels, help train dancing bears for the midnight circus over in Princessa, or even advise the king and queen of Chimera!"

I knelt down and held out my finger to a little wisp of a fairy that trotted along one of the tall yellow-green blades. "I'm sorry, Z, but if you had a point, you must remember to condense your speeches if you want me to pay attention. Can you give me the 'too long, didn't listen' version?"

"*Oh!*" Zelda jerked me upright by my cardigan and spun me around.

"My fairy!" I cried out as the little beauty took flight, but not without sticking out her tongue at Zelda. "You see that? I second the sentiment. You sound almost as bad as Percy, you know, and look where his windbag ways got him." I patted the beast, who spun his red eyes around towards us and bared his dark teeth. Or something—it really was hard to tell in his amorphous form. But that was the gist of the attitude I got from him.

"Haddie, you have to listen to me. We are going to be in big trouble for your mistake. You have to start taking responsibility for these...these brouhahas you always cause!"

"I *do* take responsibility for my mistakes," I licked my lips. "Remember when I accidentally enchanted all those creme brûlées? Who do you think spent each evening eating every one of them once you disenchanted them?"

"Oh, I'm sure having extra sweets really tore you up inside, didn't it?" Zelda sighed and took the lead as we rounded the final bend to Morgana Hall. "My point being —you have to stop being quite so careless. You probably maimed or killed poor Percy, and now we have to go to Headmistress Demetria and see if there's any way to rescue him."

"There's a way to rescue him, Zelda. There always is." I gestured to a row of pixies that perched on a birch tree, each sparkling their own unique color so that the branches were all illuminated like Christmas. "We have magic, remember? Magic can fix everything."

"YOU CAN ABSOLUTELY NOT JUST RELY on magic to fix everything!" Headmistress Demetria bellowed as she paced back and forth. The moment we'd confessed to our crimes —or, more so, my crimes—the bun that held her dark hair up seemed to unwind, and her pince-nez glasses on a string had fallen to her bosom.

She slid her hand into her hairline as she rounded the corner of her mahogany desk. "You Underwood girls have a long tradition of creating ruckuses." She gestured to the long line of portraits on the wall to our right, where equally frazzled headmistresses all stared back at us with still-life horror. "Every single one of my ancestors had an Underwood child as the bane of their existence." Head-mistress Demetria finally paused to cup Zelda's chin. "Except you, dear one. Here I thought the Underwoods finally had a white sheep in their family, but *you*…" She whirled on me. "*You* cause enough hubbub for all your generation combined! And *eating* my *son*! Oh!"

She collapsed back against her desk and accidentally made her large collection of enchanted feathered pencils fall over. Free from their bonds, they zoomed around the room like they were free birds once more.

"I apologize profusely for my sister's actions today. We recognize that she is incorrigible and tends to rush headlong into her latest schemes without thinking." Zelda tilted her head down at me, but I only pointed up to the ceiling.

"Look—" I started, until Zelda booted me in the shin. "*Ow*! I mean—yes. Okay. Whatever it takes to rescue Percy, that's what we'll do." I glared at my taller sister. "I'm awfully sorry about everything, too. But don't you think the *real* lesson here is how dangerous lectures can be? I mean, if Percy hadn't been so intent on his role as disciplinarian, it's possible he could still be with us—"

"Haddie!" Zelda smacked me upside the head. "Can you stop and show some sympathy for once in your life?"

"Yes, ma'am," I ducked my head. "How can I help fix this terrible, terrible tragedy?"

Another kick from Zelda.

"What? I said it was a terrible tragedy!"

"You look like you're going to laugh!"

I stifled a cackle. "Okay, but it's not every day you get to see a boy be eaten by a giant monster of darkness!"

Zelda smothered my mouth. "I'm really sorry about her, Headmistress Demetria. I don't know what went wrong."

"The whole Underwood family," Headmistress Demetria moaned. "That's what went wrong." She pinched her nose together and shooed us out. "If you wouldn't mind leaving that sleeping...*thing*...behind, I need to run some tests to see what you unleashed upon us. I'll call you back in once I've determined our next course of action."

From the right-hand corner of the office, right under the horrified headmistresses of years past, my beast let out a snore as it pawed at the red rug underneath it.

Zelda curtseyed, and her grip on me meant that I was forced to do the same. "Yes, Headmistress Demetria. We, of course, will pray for the best as we await your decision."

"THIS—IS—THE—WORST—DECISION—*EVER*." I gritted my teeth as I stared at the lumbering behemoth I'd created. "You mean I have to go *in there*? I don't fancy getting eaten by a monster this century, thank you very much!"

I'd barely had a few hours to relax and eat dinner before Headmistress Demetria called me back to her office. My stomach grumbled, and, in one way, I was jealous of my creation. At least he'd had a well-rounded meal as of late, and, by the way things were going, I'd be his second course.

"Oh, let's be honest, Haddie Underwood. You'd get eaten by a monster sooner or later." Headmistress Demetria nudged me a little bit closer. "Your teachers and I have studied it, and the best we can figure is that you have somehow connected this beast to the Underworld through some terrible manipulation. I'd ask you how you did it, but I'm afraid it was your sheer idiocy that led us here."

"Careful, Headmistress Demetria. I might start to think you care for me." I crouched down and looked in the gaping maw of the sleeping beast. "He seems so nice and cheerful right now—are you sure you want to ruin his nappy-poo? Percy can stay down in the Underworld for a few more...years. Or so."

Zelda rolled her green eyes. "*Haddie.*"

"Okay! Okay." I took a deep gulp and adjusted my satchel. A wand, a light stone, and a loaf of bread were inside. "I feel awfully unprepared for this, though, and I don't know whether it's on purpose because you hold a grudge towards me, or just because you don't want to lose anything important should I get stuck in there."

"Like my son?" Headmistress Demetria raised her thin eyebrows. "Remember, the light stone will guide you. On the way down, it will help you find Percy. Once you've got him, only by following its rays can you ever exit the Underworld again." She undid the satchel once more. "The wand—well, no need to explain that. But remember, don't eat any food that grows in the Underworld, or else you'll be stuck there forever. And you must find Percy before he eats anything. Do you understand?"

"Yes, yes, I understand! You've only repeated it several hundred times." I waved her away, only for Zelda to take her place in my face.

"Yes, and aren't you the one always harping on your attention deficit? Excuse me if we want to make sure that you are paying attention to all of this."

I twisted up my lips. "I've got it, Z. Use the wand for obvious things like magic. Use the food because I don't want to die. And use the light stone to find my way. Got it, got it." I shoved her away. "Well, I'll see you all soon, right?"

I dropped down on all fours, sucked in a breath, and crawled into the open maw of my creation.

"They're both doomed," I heard Headmistress Demetria say right before the portal sucked me into its embrace.

"*Doom!*" someone bellowed in the darkness. "All who enter here are doomed!"

I blinked my eyes to try and adjust to the sudden lack of light, but when that failed, I scrounged about in my bag until I found my wand. My fingers tightened around its carved oak surface—I'd taken the plain, chunky piece of wood that we'd all been given at orientation and turned it into a masterpiece, complete with dancing unicorns, fairies, and centaurs, all in a forest setting.

Of course, I wasn't a very good carver, so Zelda complained I'd turned a respectable wizarding tool into a kindergarten art project, but regardless. The crystal core could still amplify and focus my magical power, which was what I needed it to do.

"*Illuminate!*" I snapped my fingers and it reacted to my command.

"Doom, doom, doom, doom," several other voices cried out. I held the wand aloft but didn't see anything on the road in front of me.

"Turn around," one wailed. "Turn around before you see Charon! For once he has you in his clutches, there's naught to do but go straight to Cerberus's teeth!"

"Sorry, already crawled in the muzzle of one creature today. Don't fancy doing it again for a while." I inched forward until I felt something wet against my shoes. I yelped and hopped away from—from—

I lowered my wand and saw black waves as they tumbled on the sand.

"Where is this place?" I asked the voices. "That is, if you can bring yourself to say something other than *doom*."

"The River Cocytus," someone answered.

"Bless you," I muttered as I held out my wand and willed the light to go brighter. I could see vague, shadowy outlines, one of which looked just like an…

An arm.

It reached up for me, inky and watery, just like it was made from the depths of the River Cockatoo itself, or whatever the doomsayer had called it.

"Percy!" I screamed. "Perce, where are you?"

"He's doomed," one of the voices said. "As are you."

"Thank you, but do you mind giving me a second opinion?" I hopped back and forth on my feet and pulled out my light stone to check to make sure I was even going in the right direction. Of course, the yellow beam that it emitted would lead right across the river of hands.

"I sure hope you're worth this someday, Percy." I gritted my teeth, tucked the light stone into my bag, and extended my wand once more. "*Freeze*!"

A beam of ice shot from its tip. I could hear the crackle of the river as it froze over and see the vague outlines through the faint glow of the light stone through my bag.

I took a deep breath, and—

Screamed as I plunged across the ice at a haphazard pace. My feet slipped as I crashed to the ice and skidded a few paces. I clung to my wand as nightmarish scenes danced across my mind, visions of it sliding into the murky depths below, gone forever. Unfortunately, my little accident also made my pathway turn wonky as it suddenly swooped dramatically to the left...and my body slipped straight ahead.

I caught my breath one moment before I entered the River Cock-a-doodle-doo.

"Doom!" someone screamed in my ear.

I flailed as arms groped at me and dragged me down, down, down. Fighting with Zelda had left me well-prepared for fistfights, but even my sharp elbows couldn't make contact. Every other body seemed to be made of nothing but liquid.

"You are doomed to join us!"

I writhed while my wand shot hectic beams in various directions. The saltwater stung at my eyes and all I wanted to do was clench them tight to guard against the pain.

Lungs. Burned. No. Air.

Panic tried to creep in and fill my heart just as the water tried to fill my lungs, but I refused to let it in. No—I needed clarity and confidence because fear had never saved anyone. Ask any hero or heroine in a horror novel.

I snapped the wand behind me, towards the faint outlines that I could feel being handsy with me. I froze the fingers as their grips tightened.

I'd have none of that doom and dying stuff, thank you very much. I hacked off the limbs of my attackers with my arms and legs as soon as they were solid enough to touch.

Freeze. Smash. Freeze. Smash. Lungs. Dying.

No panic. No fear. No time.

I scrounged at the makeshift rope my ice had created and hoisted myself upwards.

Vision fading.

Hands slipping.

Maybe I was doomed after all.

Or maybe…

I could fight…

I had *magic*.

I stuck the end of the wand into my mouth and air exploded into my lungs as I mentally cast an oxygen spell.

Breathe in through my mouth. Climb. Kick.

Agony.

But at last, my hand pierced the current and grabbed onto the top of the sheet of ice. My nails dug into the grooves as I hauled myself up and over.

I spluttered up the black, salty water. My wand fell out of my mouth and I rolled on top of it to keep it secure.

Safe.

A boatman rowed up beside me as I heaved up whatever goo my stomach had created.

"Need a ride on the River Cocytus?" A hooded man stood next to the bow, a solitary lantern on his staff. "I'll take you over to the River Acheron for a small fee."

"Doom!" one of the wailers cried. "There is only doom ahead!"

I fished my light stone out from my bag and held it up. It didn't seem any dimmer in comparison to the stranger's lamp, nor did it falter in the direction.

I needed to go straight to find Percy.

"Thanks, but no thanks." I scooped up my wand and began to freeze the waves once more. "I know what I have to do."

The ferryman drifted forward. "Pay my toll, and I will take you to your destination."

"Like I said..." I reached the other side of the river and hopped onto the shore. I gave the man a two-fingered salute as I pranced off in the direction of the light. "I don't think your destination is anywhere I want to go."

"TELL me again why I'd want to go anywhere for Percy Holmes? I'll probably find him and the first thing he'll say is, 'I'm writing you up because your shirt is not properly tucked into your skirt and your socks are not perfectly even. Tut-tut, Miss Underwood. With a track record like this, you're on grounds to expulsion.'"

I tucked my wand and light stone back into my bag as little glowing trees illuminated my path instead. On every branch hung a glowing pomegranate—so red that they looked like blood itself.

My stomach rumbled just at the sight of them, and I dug through my bag to find the bread I'd started the journey with. I pulled apart a piece and grimaced as the water-logged food stuck to my fingers.

"Percy?" I called softly in the darkness. "Percy, I'm really sorry my little experiment ate you. I think you gave him indigestion, though, so I would say it's about even. Wouldn't you say?" I paused and tilted my head. There was no sound. It was like I was trapped in a void, without even the river behind me. Almost like the darkness that had engulfed me before, but this time, it blocked out my hearing.

"Percy?"

You're so hungry, Haddie. Eat us. Eat just one of us. We will fill you forever.

Instead of the voice of the head prefect, I caught wind of the small whispers of...the fruits.

My mouth started to drool, and I wiped it away with the collar of my cardigan. But with each command, the hole in my stomach only seemed to gnaw further and further into my innards. If I didn't eat, and soon, there would be nothing left of me. I would only be a hollow woman, a skeleton walking.

My feet faltered, and I rested a hand on one of the trees. Right above me bloomed the most exquisite, perfect example of fruit known to man….

I lifted a finger. Stroked the skin. My hands circled around its plump form.

You're so close to one bite, Haddie. Just a little more, and you can be one with us. Stay with us...be the queen of this land...just one bite, Haddie. This is why the Underwoods have never fit in with the rest of the magical world. You were meant to be here...we are your destiny. Here, you will find all your hopes and dreams when you seize the Underwood destiny that so many of your ancestors have been running from.

Yes. Yes, that had to be true. My family had never fit in anywhere—well, Zelda did, but she was an anomaly. We were the ruffians, the miscreants, the adventurers that never seemed to calm down. This was my destiny. I would be Queen of the Underworld…

A pain seized my stomach, and I doubled over. My hands shook as I ripped open the flap of my bag and began to stuff the crumbling bits of bread into my mouth. I gagged from the sheer amount of salt, but with each bite, I seemed to regain my tether to reality—and remembered why one should never listen to talking fruit.

I took a deep breath and righted myself. "Percy? Percy Holmes, I'm sorry that I told you that you never shut up. If you can hear me now, it's as good a time as any to start in on a lecture. I don't know if my tie exactly matches my socks. Isn't that a travesty? Don't you just want to tear me into pieces? Tell me what a burden to society I am?"

Oh, come on. That was *always* one of his favorite lecture topics.

I switched gears. "Percy, I seem to have forgotten some of Morgana Hall's hallowed history. Would you mind reciting your dissertation on it, complete with why we have a semi-dead corpse of King Arthur? I know you've told me a thousand times because it's *super* important to the past and future of Kingland, but I usually lose interest right about the time you open your mouth. Some bit about Merlin…something about Morgana…is Arthur really dead, or is he merely unconscious? Have we tried getting a princess in here to lay one on him to see if the spell will break? I'm probably way off track here. Don't you want to correct me?"

I paused. Listened. Intentionally drowned out the blasted, pushy pomegranates.

And then I heard it.

"Haddie?"

"Percy! Oh, thank goodness!" I veered off the path and into the brambles that surrounded the glowing trees. With each step, the forest seemed to grow taller and taller, until their tops looked like stars decorating the night sky.

But once I reached the center, the perfectionist prefect wasn't there.

I turned around in a circle. "Perce? Are you hiding? Really, it's not funny…"

A shadow, barely visible in the dim light, darted behind the glittering trunks. Dark foliage crunched underneath my feet as I approached it. "Percy, if that's you—I swear. Come out right now."

"Haddie?" Again, the voice sounded like Percy, but

the shadow never stopped moving. "Haddie Underwood, is that you?"

I lost sight of the ghost, only to feel a chill creep up my shoulders and send a tremor down my spine, all the way to my toes. I whirled around, but whatever had been there had disappeared already.

"You're not Percy."

"How do you know? You never really knew Percy to begin with. You never took the time to truly get to know him."

The voice sounded familiar, but at the same time, I couldn't identify it. My brain seemed to revolt at its very existence.

"I don't know what you mean. Percy is Percy. He's Percy Holmes, upright prefect who's never had a bit of fun in his life. Know-it-all, killjoy, rambles about everything for no discernable reason..." I crossed my arms over my chest. "But I'd still like him back, if it's all the same to you. I'm pretty sure getting the Headmistress' son turned into a snack is grounds for expulsion."

The voice scoffed. "That's all you're worried about, isn't it? Yourself. How *you* might be affected if Percy stayed here."

I glared at the darkness. "Oh, don't go mangling my words and try to pin this on me. Everything that happened was an *accident*. I'm here to make it right. Of course Perce wants out. What else is there to know?"

The voice hummed. I felt another cold breeze ruffle my skirt and the ends of my brown hair. I smacked at my legs and clenched my knees together. "And what are you? Some kind of perverted phantom?"

The branches ruffled against each other, which seemed to amplify the pomegranates' voices—or whatever that was.

"I see you, little girl."

"I'm not *little*." I tilted my nose and examined the gigantic trees. "And I don't have time to waste on you anymore." I pulled out the light stone. Blast it all—I'd gotten so distracted that I ran off course. The light went straight behind me and veered to the left.

I pivoted and marched out of the woods. Or at least, that was my intention. Brambles cut at my legs and the wind buffeted me backward and tore at my supply satchel. I held up my arms to defend against it but still found myself driven against the trunk of a tree.

"Leave without Percy and nothing will happen to you in the Underworld," the spectre that spoke to me earlier whispered in my ear. "You have no business here. He is mine."

"Fat lot. If I come back without him, Zelda and Headmistress Demetria will murder me."

The voice lowered into a snarl. "Fine. Do what you will—but I'll set the whole Underworld against you."

The wind vanished. The chatty foods above my head fell silent. But dread still seized my foot as I tried to take my first step.

A large howl made the top of the branches rattle. I tottered and tipped forward onto my knees on almost the exact same spot that I'd banged against the ice—absolutely perfect. A broken kneecap would be the only thing to make the day better.

A tree crashed somewhere near me, and I rolled

down a small embankment until my side caught against a rock.

A massive, dark brown dog loomed over me—smaller than the trees themselves, but that wasn't saying much.

But the most important detail, even more than its size, was the fact that it had three heads all aimed directly at me, teeth bared.

Dogs. Why did it always have to be dogs?

"I HATE DOGS!" I screeched as I clambered upright. My shoe caught on the rock and I almost took a third dive but somehow managed to remain standing.

From somewhere behind me, I thought I heard the cackle of my disembodied torturer.

"After her, Cerberus!"

If only Zelda had come with me. She'd somehow manage to tame this mutt all while taunting me that I didn't have anything to fear. That I needed to conquer my childish phobias. No matter how many times I brought up our Aunt Selene's yippy, snapping dog, Zelda just never could understand the trauma of being bit by a canine. Never mind that I had the scar on my calf to prove the danger. She was convinced all puppies were harmless and cute.

I doubted even Cerberus could change her mind.

The trees grew smaller around me as I retraced my steps on the trail of the light stone. I clutched it in my fist as the thin beam poured out from between my fingers.

Two thoughts drowned out every single sense: *don't lose the stone* and *don't fall or get eaten*.

Somehow, I didn't think I'd be as lucky as Percy if Cerberus made supper out of *me*.

The trees bent and snapped underneath the weight of his giant paws. I needed to hide, I needed to use magic, I needed to fight—but my brain couldn't process anything quickly enough to put any of these ideas into action. Stupid panic and fear—like I said, they'd never helped anyone. They just threatened to dull my brain and my oodles of self-assurance, which was what I really needed.

I vaulted over a small bush and prayed my skirt would clear it as well. I landed on my feet, staggered a few inches, and managed to steady myself. The shine from the trees dimmed as I got closer back to my initial path, but that meant there was less resistance for Cerberus in his pursuit.

Now.

Do or die.

I *needed* my wand.

I skidded to my left when the light stone directed me to and trusted the path would be straight if I swapped it out for my wand.

There was no time to remember the perfect spell. I couldn't triple-check my thoughts or make sure I used the right incantation or whatnot. Pure, unbridled instinct guided me as I fished my weapon out from my satchel and whirled around for my final stand.

"Stop! *Stop, stop, stop!*" I shook my wand at the beast. An explosion of power sent me spiraling backward like Cerberus himself had hit me. My body slammed into the ground and my one tiny twig of protection rolled away from me.

I rolled over several times before I came to a stop. My head lolled for a second, but it was hard to judge if my vision was fading since everything was already so dark to begin with.

Cerberus howled again, and though Zelda would swear it was psychosomatic, I *knew* my scar started to burn.

"Leave the Underworld and I'll call him off," the vaguely familiar voice taunted. I could almost put my finger on it, but still, the speaker eluded me. Definitely female, though. How had I ever mistaken it for Percy?

"And if I leave, I leave Percy behind. No thanks." I tried to prop myself up, but I just needed a few more seconds. Really—I wouldn't pass out.

"Your little stun spell is about to wear off. It takes triple the magic to control Cerberus," the girl snickered. "I bet you probably want your wand right about now, don't you?"

"I can do hand magic."

"It takes a lot more magic to halt Cerberus than someone like *you* can conjure up without a crystal conduit. Maybe if Percy were here...or...let's see...yes, your sister, Zelda. I'm sure she could do it, couldn't she?"

I could hear something that sounded like cracking in the direction of Cerberus. My stupid, weak arms refused to cooperate and lift me off the ground.

Okay, we'd revisit the topic of getting up in a second. I crawled forward, though my body protested that, too. But I would sure protest more if I died.

A bit more.

I pressed forward and scrounged about. I could sense a chill at my back. It urged me to give up without words, to settle down, or turn around. Any option would suit it except the one where I found my wand, conquered Cerberus, and rescued Percy.

Cerberus howled. An initial head started the cry, but the other two soon rallied around it, and I could feel the ground tremor as they worked out the last bits of the stupor I'd cast.

"Come on...come on..." I muttered. *"Illuminate!"*

Right by the edge of the forest, my wand burst into life.

"You beautiful thing, you!" My feet slipped as I tried once more to run towards it. I crashed and crawled the few final feet until my hand tightened on its carved wooden surface.

Perhaps it was all in my head, but I could have sworn just touching it gave me the fire to defend myself. I shoved myself upwards and whirled around. The snarling maw of Cerberus loomed right in front of me, all three heads poised to strike.

"Shrink! Go small! Diminish, you big oaf!" My light cut out as my magic attempted to interpret the mashed-up instructions I'd given.

Cerberus leaned forward as I shouted more incoherent demands of my powers.

Sparks flew everywhere. All over him, all over me—they burned as they sank into my skin, and Cerberus yowled and scratched his heads in turn.

"Small! Shrink! De-grow!" I continued.

More and more specks wrapped themselves around Cerberus and tightened themselves into a whip. Each head attacked another as the magic lifted him off the ground, spun him around, and deposited him back on the ground.

Only now, he was the size of a teacup.

I collapsed onto my bottom and ran my hand down my face as Cerberus gnawed at my shoe.

"Even at that size you're annoying," I muttered. And though the Wizards and Witches for Animal Protection might have arrested me had they been there, I picked up the little yapper and chucked him as far as I could in the direction I'd come from. "There. I faced your stupid challenge," I called to the blackness above. "As you can see, nothing you throw at me can stop me from finding Percy."

———

"WHY DON'T YOU STOP?"

I sneezed once as I tramped through a field full of red flowers. I shook off the hand of a blissful youth that grabbed at my ankle as he reclined on the ground. His face had an unnatural golden glow to it. For some reason, unlike in the other parts of the Underworld, this place was lit up as if it was a summer day. Not exactly with sunshine, but from an indiscernible light source.

"I've got to find my friend, that's why." I chewed on another limp, crushed piece of bread. I could hardly choke it down, but it at least helped steel my appetite against the distant call of the pomegranates.

"But you should stop and play!" a teenage girl called.

She, too, radiated like the boy. Come to think of it, every single body I could spot in the fields did.

"You deserve it. You've struggled for so long—why don't you just come and rest for a moment?" A different girl lifted a languid hand. "Come and relax in the Elysian Fields. All your labors will just...disappear." She giggled as she fell back into a clump of buttercups.

"You could join us for a bit of revelry," another boy agreed. He tugged at my satchel, and I slapped him away.

"No. Not until I find Percy. He's my friend."

"Ah, such friendship that sends one into the depths of the Underworld. Not since Merlin and Arthur have we seen anything like it." I gave up trying to discern who spoke. All the fair-haired youths looked much too alike. Too unearthly.

"Why are you so determined to find him? What has he ever done for you?"

That voice stuck out to me if only because it lacked the melodic overtones of the rest of the people.

I stopped. "Oh. I was wondering when you would show back up."

The wind buffeted me once more. "Ever since you've been here, I've been picking up little bits and pieces of you. And I frankly can't see why you're so determined."

"I've *answered*," I growled. "You just don't listen. Because if I don't get Perce out of here, I'll be expelled."

"Yes, yes. So you say. But you can hardly stand school to begin with. You mostly just goof off." The zephyr buffeted my hair around and into my face. "Would it really be that big of a loss?"

"Would it?" the languid youths cried as they tugged at

my socks. Somehow, someone managed to slip one of my shoes off. "Just come play with us. Forget about it."

"I—can't just...I mean…" I swallowed. My throat felt lumpy, and I sneezed again. "I *enjoy* school. I enjoy magic. I like finding new and unique ways to apply things. Like—back with Cerberus. Or when I created my little monster. That was really fun until I ended up here."

"But do you really *learn* anything there? You mostly seem to teach yourself. You just said so—you're an *instinctual* learner. What can those teachers give you? Like Headmistress Demetria. She's much more suited to teach people like Zelda. People who excel academically with a rigid structure." The flower children wrestled me to the ground with the help of the wind.

As soon as my body landed, the atmosphere seemed to change. The flowers seemed hazier but yet brighter. The smell seemed softer and sweeter, not quite as irritating to my nose, and my eyelids fell to half-mast.

Maybe they were right. I just needed a little bit of sleep. After all, my eyes were so heavy. And I'd fought off river people *and* Cerberus. I deserved just a teensy bit of a respite.

I settled down. No bed ever felt quite so plush or smelled as delicious—buttercups mixed with rain, like a spring bouquet.

I wasn't giving in—or even giving up. I was...recuperating. I would stay in school. I would rescue Percy. I just needed a little time for myself first. That wouldn't *doom* anyone, right?

THE WIND'S cackling woke me up. "You've doomed Percy!"

I started awake and found myself not in a field of flowers, but back on the strange path, surrounded by trees full of pomegranates.

"I have not!" I yelled into the nighttime. "I'm getting him right now."

I jerked my shoes back on and staggered to my feet.

"Oh, no," the voice said. "Don't you realize? It's too late."

Why did she sound so blasted familiar?

The shadow trailed a cold hand along my neck. I imagined that it circled me like a vulture with its prey.

"I realized something after my first two challenges. Your worst enemy isn't your phobias or sheer manpower. No...your worst enemy, Haddie Underwood, is yourself."

My tormentor slowly materialized in front of me—a faded twin version of myself. Everything about the copy was dimmer, like she was covered in shadows.

I blinked. Fire raced down my back as I stared at this doppelganger. My face grew warm, and I curled my left hand into a fist.

Now that just wouldn't do. For better or for worse, there was only *one* Haddie Underwood, and this—this *Fake-Haddie* would never be her.

"You're so confident in whatever choice you make that you never realize the consequences. You were determined to find Percy so that *you* didn't get expelled from school," Fake-Haddie smirked. "But you never gave a thought to what the Underworld's plan was for *Percy*. Or that he might be enduring the same challenges without any assistance."

I whipped out my wand and leveled it at Fake-Haddie. "*Illuminate attack!*"

I chucked a ball of light at her, but she stepped over to dodge it. "All I had to do was distract you for a little bit. I may not have been able to get you to succumb and be the next life force of the Underworld, but Percy?" she shrugged. "Well, he was simple enough, if only because he didn't know *anything.*"

Fake-Haddie glided over to a large tree, where a slumped-over form sat.

"Perce!" I rushed forward and grabbed his cheeks. I could hear his subtle breathing, but he didn't stir as I touched him. Blood seeped out of his mouth. "*Percy Holmes!*"

Blast it all. The fire I'd stoked inside of me smothered under an avalanche of ice.

I'd done this.

All of Percy's lecturing and warnings about how one day, I'd end up doing something irreversible and awful…

Ugh. I hated the cold inside me. It drove me to slap him across the face. "*Perce*! Wake up!"

"Oh, don't bother," Fake-Haddie nudged a half-eaten pomegranate out of the way. Red stained Percy's hands as well. "He ate. By the rules of magic, he is now connected to the Underworld." Fake-Haddie spread her arms out wide. "All of *this* survives because of the unintentional sacrifice of millions of *stupid* mortals."

"Perce!" I gave him a few rough shakes. "Percy, wake up. *Now*. If—if you don't, I swear I'm going to cause trouble. I'm going to do something bad, and who's going to stop me?"

"You, of course, were my first desire, since you're an Underwood. I've longed to lure one unsuspecting Underwood down here for centuries. Always in the upper worlds, but they never quite fit in. Always too rambunctious, too daring...don't you just know that you're meant to be down here, with me?" Fake-Haddie gestured to the Underworld around her. "What about you? You've never quite fit in at Morgana Hall, anyway. I could teach you how to use that unbridled magic of yours for some real chaos."

"I don't want to cause your kind of chaos. Oh, sure, *normal* chaos is fun when it happens, but this...this is not what I want." I snapped my fingers in front of Percy's face. "What I *want* is Percy Holmes released back to the—whatever you called it. Real-world, real-life, upper-world, who cares."

"But you could be Queen of the Underworld, Haddie." Fake-Haddie knelt down beside me. "You and I...we're so similar." Fake-Haddie held up her arm against mine as if we were comparing suntans. "It's why your skin is such a good fit for me," she tittered. "Your magic could keep me alive for millennia, especially if we could lure others in as well. The dead would answer to you alone, and soon enough, we could storm the upper worlds and let the beautiful darkness of the Underworld be free."

"No way in—in the Underworld I'm letting you get out." I spun around, fist already raised to punch the imposter in the face, but she vanished before my knuckles could make contact with her lips.

She reappeared a few feet away, her visage twisted into a sneer. "You never listen, do you?"

"It's one of my best qualities." I faced Percy again and pinched his cheek. "Just ask Perce."

I could feel Fake-Haddie's presence close in on me until her icy breath was next to my ear. "I doubt you'll be asking Percy anything ever again. I'm going to use him as an imbecilic puppet and drain him dry...all because of you."

"You will *not*!" I snarled. "You give him to me!"

"Oh, I can't. That's simply not possible," Fake-Haddie smirked and leaned forward until we were almost nose-to-nose. "You lost. When you fell asleep in the Elysian Fields, it gave me just enough time to weaken Percy's resistance. He's mine now. He belongs to the Underworld."

"No!" I tried to hoist Percy up, but he had several inches and pounds on me. "That's not true."

"But, Haddie..." Fake-Haddie jerked him off me, and I staggered forward. "Percy *wants* to stay here."

My fingers almost grasped him, but Fake-Haddie wrenched him away.

I balled up my fists instead. "He does not! Who in their right mind would *want* to stay here?!"

"Why don't we ask him?" Fake-Haddie took a step back. Percy stayed upwards, like he was suspended by her strings. "You have treated poor Percy like an object for so long. Don't you think that it's time you gave him his own choice?"

She held up her hands as vines began to wrap around my feet. I tore them away and stomped on them. "Percy— Percy, listen to me! I can get us out of the Underworld."

Fake-Haddie yawned. "Oh, be serious. You can't get

both of you out of here. One of you must stay to feed the Underworld now. That's how the magic of the pomegranates works."

I lunged out for that stupid head prefect. "Please, Percy! I'm—I'm *sorry*! I don't know how to change. I really don't." I kicked at more of Fake-Haddie's vines. My voice went up a notch. All the events I'd been responsible for, all the mayhem…desperation seemed to creep into my mind like an infection. "I just keep screwing things up for you. I didn't *mean* to send you to the Underworld. I swear! Just like I didn't mean to create that monster…and I didn't mean to create sentient desserts…and…I didn't mean to make every left shoe in Morgana Hall go missing…things just *happen*, okay?" I clawed at the ground, but the vines only curled up around my arms. I growled and slashed at them with my nails.

The juice of the bloody pomegranate dribbled from Percy's lips and down his neck until it stained his collar.

"Why don't we get Percy's side of the story? After all, you're always *so* self-absorbed. You only think of yourself and what a lark life could be for you, Haddie Underwood." Fake-Haddie shoved Percy towards me. He blinked his hollow eyes once before his mouth moved in stiff spasms.

"On your first day, you exploded a potion that turned the hair of several nearby students into various hues. I spent the rest of the day cleaning up the rainbow stains from everything in that room—including the ceiling —under my mother's watchful eye. That's what a good headmaster does, she said."

I winced. "Percy…" I reached for him, but he was still out of my grasp, a writhing wall of plants between us.

"You didn't even offer to help. I had to stay up past midnight to clean it up, and the next morning, you called me a teacher's pet when my mother applauded me in front of the school." Percy stared straight ahead. "I was so embarrassed. Others started picking on me too, then. They said that I only got good grades because of who my mother was. That I was a kiss-up. Every time I fixed another one of your messes, I only got teased more and more."

"Well—that is—I mean—" I spluttered. I'd never really...*meant* any of those things I said about Percy. It was just the jocular nature of our relationship. I'd thought...

What had I thought?

Nothing?

"Eventually, when my mother made me prefect, the others bullied me about that, too. Not you. You're always so oblivious, but you don't realize the way your capers affect others. You think they're all in good fun—that it's just how quirky and lovable you are." Blood tears leaked out of the corners of Percy's gray eyes. They trailed down his nose and past his lips before they plopped onto the ground. Tiny pomegranate trees began to sprout as they did. "They said that I hadn't done anything to earn the position. That I was just mummy's favorite little boy. So I set out to prove I *did* deserve it. I hammered down on all the rules and tiny infractions to make a point to everyone that I deserved to be prefect, and not just because of my name or my future role at Morgana Hall." The red blobs fell faster. Soon enough, Percy would have his own miniature forest as a cage.

"And when I earned a promotion to head prefect, even you got more attitude with me. Then it seemed like you did things to purposely incite me. You summoned hobgoblins 'by accident,' you '*somehow*' gave me a stomach bug...you turned me into an infant in one of your cauldron potions gone wrong."

And it had all seemed pretty hilarious at the time. I remembered laughing hysterically as Baby Percy wailed. We'd all passed him around the room until Headmistress Demetria had come and aged him back up to his proper size.

But now...

I pursed my lips and furrowed my brow so that no blasted tears would leak out. I didn't remember the last time I'd cried—maybe the day my aunt's brutish dog bit me. Haddie Underwood did not whimper or sniffle or wail.

"And after all that...why would I want to go with you?" Percy's fists clenched—the first twitch of movement I had seen from him in a while.

I gritted my teeth and jerked at my restraints, which were blurry with the weight of so many unshed tears. "Because I'm trying to save you, Percy!" The sparkling trees grew up higher and higher. Soon, he'd be locked in them, nothing but a caged bird.

"Maybe this is freedom," Percy whispered. "Freedom from *you*."

Oh.

Ouch.

"*Stop!*" I shrieked.

Both Fake-Haddie and Percy blinked.

"I know...I know I've been a terror." The quiet words fell from my lips. I could still feel the fire inside of me, but it had morphed somehow. Turned into something I didn't recognize—maybe fueled by…

Guilt? No, that wasn't right.

Could it be I actually felt a teeny, tiny bit of genuine repentance as I examined my deeds through Percy's eyes?

"I'm sorry that I got you in trouble so much, and I'm sorry my beast took you to the Underworld," I sniffed as the dam I'd built on my tear ducts started to leak. I wiped them away but remembered to examine them; no use trapping myself in a cage because I had to blubber for the first time in years. But the droplets were still clear as I scrutinized them on my finger. "I know this is all my fault, so let me fix it. Percy didn't know not to eat the food. It's not right that he has to be stuck down here as a prisoner."

"What's your point?" Fake-Haddie tapped her nails against her skin.

I sucked in a breath and waited for my next few heartbeats to pass. I brushed the rest of my tears away as they fell.

"Let him go. A fair trade, yeah? I'll stay behind and give power to the Underworld." I rolled up my sleeves like I was ready should they jab an IV into my arm right now to leech me dry. "You can use all my blood, all my lifeforce, my magic, whatever it is that you're sucking from Percy. This is *my fault*."

Fake-Haddie sneered. "You have no idea what you're offering, you little brat."

"Maybe not, but I do pay attention to some of my lessons. I know you can't refuse it." Actually, I hadn't technically learned that from a lesson. During one of my first tours of Morgana Hall, back before I'd even officially started, Percy had lectured about that very topic. He'd stood in front of King Arthur's corpse and recited all the laws about trading one's life for a friend, and how profound that magic is. "Self-sacrificial magic cannot be undone. It's a bond written so deeply into the rules that it permeates everything. And I'm offering myself for Percy. His contract with you is *over*."

Fake-Haddie rolled her eyes. "Fine. You realize, though, that this solves nothing? I wanted you all along. In every sense, this is a victory for me."

She waved her hand, and the plants that had ensnared me crumbled. Percy's trees shriveled and dried, the last sparks extinguishing in the dirt, and he coughed and lurched forward.

He wiped at his eyes and mouth and yelped as he saw the residue that came away. His face swiveled between me and Fake-Haddie until I grabbed him and gave him a good shake.

"Look here. Look at me. She's not real. She's just a representation of my worst enemy," I took a deep breath in order to fortify my internal dam again. Yes—maybe I was my own worst enemy, but, as far as I was concerned, I could also be my own hero—and Percy's, too.

I jostled him once more. "I'm sorry for sending you here, Perce. Tell everyone that I'm okay."

"Remember the deal," Fake-Haddie crowed. A tiny pomegranate tree sprouted right next to me, and my stomach rumbled in desperation.

"I *know*," I snarled at her. "Can it for one second, you bad imitation." I licked my lips and passed my satchel to him, but not before I withdrew the light stone. "Here. This light will guide you out. Don't turn from the path it shows you, and don't eat any other food here. There's soggy left-over bread, and I'm sorry it's all I can give you. There's a wand in there, which you know how to use better than I do, anyway."

My voice trailed off after that. I wanted to give him greetings for Zelda, to tell her that she really was the best sister in the world. I knew she'd miss me, if only because she wouldn't have a human punching bag anymore. Head-mistress Demetria...deep down, she'd probably miss me, too, just as much as I'd miss her—no need to clarify how much or little that was.

I sucked in a deep breath, but Percy cut in before I could tell my final goodbyes. "I don't understand, Haddie. Why are you acting like you're not coming with me? I mean—you came in here to rescue me, I assume? It's all fuzzy, but I remember..."

"It's a bad lot, that's all. Only one of us can escape."

Percy's thin brows furrowed in confusion. "But...why?"

"Because you ate one of my pomegranates and thus became the new lifeforce of the Underworld." Fake-Haddie batted her eyelashes at him and gestured to the new pome-granate, which was plump and juicy right beside me. "Haddie has offered to take your place instead, and by the laws of magic, I can't refuse her offer."

"*Haddie!*" Percy gaped at me. "Why?"

"Oh, don't listen to her. We both know you wouldn't even be in the Underworld if it wasn't for me," I rolled my eyes. "This is my burden, Percy. I'm just telling you—don't let them forget me. And if they want to erect a statue of me in memoriam, please make sure that I at least look more attractive than the ugly bearded dude in town."

"I can't let—" Percy began.

I put my finger over his lips to shush him. "Let's be honest. When have you ever been able to tell me what I could or couldn't do?"

Then, before he could get any original ideas, I grabbed the fruit and bit into it. Blood rolled down my lips and into my collar, and I felt my body stiffen as my mind went foggy.

"Stop!" Percy yelled through the haze. "There has to be *something* I can do!"

"She's bound to the Underworld," Fake-Haddie shrugged. "There's nothing to do—"

"No—I know!" Percy grabbed my hand. I was just as frozen as he had been previously, and I hardly felt it as he dug out my wand and sliced open our palms with a quick spell. "You really should pay attention when I talk, Haddie. I told you about this on the first day you came to Morgana Hall, back on that tour."

Clouds rolled in my brain as his words blurred together. I heard them, but they held no meaning to me: Morgana Hall? Tours? All were inconsequential. There was only the Underworld.

"*I bind our essences together. Blood for blood, half for half, now and forever.*"

Pain seared against my hand, like little shocks of electricity that radiated from the cut and up into my heart. There they traveled through every vein until it felt like I was on fire—but at least I could move again.

I hacked up a bit of blood and wiped the remnants away from my lips. "Percy—"

"There." Percy straightened his back and helped me to my feet before he addressed Fake-Haddie again. "I don't know what you are, exactly, but you should know of the bond of Arthur and Merlin. When Arthur died and was brought to the Underworld, Merlin gave up half his essence to stall Arthur's death."

Fake-Haddie sneered. "Oh, and you fancy yourself a little hero, do you?"

"Not really," Percy shrugged. "Just a friend."

I blinked as the magic flowed all the way down to even my toes. "Perce, I'm really sorry, but you're going to have to rehash this one more time for me. Act as if I didn't pay attention on the tour, or to any lectures after that, because I didn't. Arthur is still dead...well, dead-ish. He's in the upper room of Morgana Hall in that coffin, awaiting the time when we need him most."

"He's *mostly* dead now, but you have to realize, he was *completely* dead." Percy gave my hand a squeeze. "Merlin brought him back from the Underworld after he'd been *murdered*. We got here accidentally through a portal, and we're both still alive. Regardless of what transpired, I think our Merlin and Arthur contract should be enough to get us out of here."

"Both of you are still bound by the Underworld. I can sense your combined essences." Fake-Haddie floated closer to us, her face caught in a sneer.

"But it's weak." I spat out a globule of saliva and saw that it was clear—for the most part. A hint of red marred it, but only a tiny sliver of one of the silver trees pushed its way up from the ground, and I squashed it beneath my feet. "I think we could leave here and you couldn't stop us, because there's just enough of each of us free to get out."

"But there's just enough trapped that you'd have to come back, eventually." Fake-Haddie stuck out her tongue, which was a good reminder for me to never do such a thing again.

Percy shrugged his shoulders. "Hmm. We each have half an essence down here, right? Which means that I'd esti- mate we'll probably have to spend half the year above ground and half a year here."

I grinned and rested my elbow on Perce's shoulder, as best as I could. "Oh, Perce, don't sell us short. I think we'd last longer. Just whenever we get to feeling—whatever we'll feel—tired or whatnot, we'll just come back down here. Set up a little winter home along the banks of the River Cockatrice until we regain our strength and can bear to be apart from this place again. And we'll come together, just so nobody gets any funny ideas about releasing the chaos of the Underworld," I paused. "And we both know it'd probably be me, so I need you to keep me in check."

Perce's gray eyes met mine, and he returned my smile. "Yeah, that sounds about right. And I'm downright sick of this place and feel rather strong myself. How do you feel, Haddie? Hale and hearty?"

I gave a sputtering cackle. "Perce, *never* use that phrase again until you're sixty-five years old, give or take. Then I think it'll be acceptable to cross your lips once more." With my free arm that didn't rest on Percy's shoulder, I flexed. "But, yes. I think I'm rather good. All my soul-bits rested and accounted for."

Fake-Haddie crossed her arms over her chest. "Think about what you've done. You'll never truly belong up there, and you'll never truly belong down here. Just eat one more pomegranate and stay down here forever." She summoned another tree with a pomegranate for each of us.

I could feel the call in the pit of my stomach once more. Percy tensed beside me, and I held him back. "No, thanks. Rather have half of a life, at least, than be stuck here as your prisoner forever." I turned to Percy. "Ready?"

He nodded and held up the light stone, which gleamed just as brightly as it ever did. "Let's go home."

———

"Oh, WELCOME HOME!" Zelda jumped on me the moment I crawled out of the beast's muzzle. "You were gone for hours." She swung me around before she deposited me back on the rug—and then slapped me upside the noggin. "I hope this finally helped one lesson sink into your thick skull."

I rubbed the spot she'd hit. "Yeah, one or two might have sunk in—if you weren't so intent on always beating them out of me, you know. Blows to the head kill brain cells."

"And she's got so few of them to spare," Percy added.

"Oh, Percy!" Headmistress Demetria cried. She threw her arms around her son and squeezed him tightly. The pièce de resistance of this atrocious display of maternal affection was a kiss to the forehead, which left a dark smudge of lipstick on Percy's olive-colored skin. "Thank goodness." She cleared her throat and adjusted her pince-nez glasses, which must have been when she spotted all the blood on Percy. "Broomsticks and baubles, Percy! What did this girl do to you?"

Percy cleared his throat and rubbed at his stained collar. "It's—it's a long story. Just…we'll explain it later."

I glanced away and twisted my face up. Or never. I was fairly certain that Headmistress Demetria wouldn't be fond of any students forging a Merlin and Arthur bond, no matter what it entailed—especially me and Percy.

"I expect a full report from both of you." Headmistress Demetria waved her spectacles at us like they were a wand that could make us both confess our adventures. When it exhibited lackluster results, she fastened them back on her face with a sniff. "Well. Haddie, I thank you for your service, even if you did almost get my boy killed in multiple ways. Now, you'll be tasked with demolishing this creature you built before it rampages again, and—"

"Wait." I held out my injured hand over the monster that had started this whole mess, though I was careful to angle my palm so my sister and Headmistress couldn't see the wound. If Headmistress Demetria saw it, I doubt she'd be as willing to drop the whole ordeal.

Somehow, I could feel the thrum of the beast's essence. Its feelings shot through my heart and settled there until I could almost hear it think. "There's no need for that. He was only scared earlier. I mean, he was essentially a newborn. His birth started with a bang and then Zelda and I just kind of…tackled him. He didn't know what to do. And he's really sorry about chowing down on Perce."

Percy studied me before he leaned out and patted the creature—well, as best as one can pet a living representation of darkness. "It's true." His voice was soft, and he gave a one-sided smile. "Can we keep him, Mum?"

Headmistress Demetria sputtered out a series of syllables that were probably intended to be excuses. Regardless, she eventually waved us out. "Oh, fine. Keep him up in one of the towers, and I do expect you to learn how to control that thing. If there is one more instance of rampaging or ingesting children, I will dismantle that thing myself, with any means necessary."

"Come on, you crazy beast." I woke the sleeping monster, and while Percy coaxed it out of the room, I threw my arms around Zelda. "I missed you. So much."

"I missed you, too." Zelda patted my head...only to spank my thigh in the next second. "Go take that creature upstairs and then come into our room and tell me what happened."

"I'll try and give you the condensed version." I gave her a peck on the cheek and darted out the door to meet Percy.

We walked in silence for the first flight of stairs, each of us with one hand over the fur of the Underworld creature.

I spoke first. "How are you feeling?"

Percy shrugged. "Okay. But—it feels like there's a sliver of me missing. Like a bit of me is stuck down there. It feels better when I'm closer to this thing, but…"

"We should give it a name!" I interjected.

Percy shot me an incredulous look. "Really? I'm trying to discuss this life-changing development with you, and…"

"Bruno. He looks like a Bruno." I slapped the rump of

the monster-thing, or whatever one would call it, and nodded. "It's settled."

Percy rolled his gray eyes. "You're still incorrigible."

"Oh, thank goodness. I'm always worried I'll change or something else terrible."

We reached the top of the staircase. In the center of the large hallway sat a dais. On top of the dais was a glass coffin, which enshrined Arthur's immaculate body.

"The bonds of friendship are keeping him alive and safe from the Underworld." I twitched my fingers together. "Just like us."

"Just like us." Percy held up his bloodied hand, and I smacked mine against it. Only, one of us lingered just a bit too long—I wasn't sure which one of us initiated it—and we ended up with our fingers plastered against each other, like we were comparing finger size.

Percy cleared his throat. "By the way...I didn't properly thank you, did I?"

I tilted my head. "Hmm. Let's see. In between lectures and life-or-death battles...no, I don't think you did."

Percy smiled, though our hands still hadn't moved. "Well, thank you. You have my deepest gratitude."

I rolled my eyes. "Oh, come *off* it. Who actually says things like that? Besides, I'm not an idiot. I'm the one that sent you there in the first place...and you're the one that initiated the Merlin and Arthur bond. So I should really be the one saying thank you."

"You're welcome."

"Ahem. I said I *should* be the one saying thank you. I didn't say I *was* saying thank you."

Percy blinked. He hadn't looked quite so shocked since Bruno devoured him.

I drew back and gave his hand another high-five. Poor Percy—he'd always be the Perciest-Perce around. "I'm kidding. Thank you."

I hopped past him and propped myself up on King Arthur's coffin. "Hmm. So, eventually, which one of us gets the pleasure of being enshrined here? Because I think I'd make a prettier semi-alive corpse, if we're being honest."

Though I assumed it broke a thousand-and-one conduct rules, Percy leaned against the glass as well. "Hopefully, neither of us. But we do have to plan. We'll have to go back to the Underworld eventually. There's no getting around that."

"Kind of like a vacation house in the Underworld, yeah?" I shrugged my shoulders. "Sounds like a relaxing getaway as it slowly drains our combined life force."

Percy cackled. "Yeah. Something like that. Maybe we should build a pool down there."

"And a juice bar! With drinks with the tiny umbrellas."

"And some cabanas."

I rapped my knuckles against King Arthur's coffin. "Think we can rent them out as prime real estate?"

"I can see our slogan now: 'The Underworld: An Escape Everyone is Dying to See.'"

I cackled, and though I'd regret it within five seconds, I stepped forward and pulled him into a hug. "Glad you're okay, Perce. Don't know what I would have done without someone here to suffer from my stupidity."

Percy tapped my back. "Glad to be back. After all,

someone's got to stop all your stupidity before it causes societal collapse."

I pulled back and slugged him in a good-natured way. "Well…if society is ever going to collapse, I'd probably be the Underwood to blame."

So, no, there wasn't an instruction manual on how to navigate this strange new development. But Percy and I—we could handle it. After all, we had Bruno, shared life essence, friendship, and magic.

Maybe one day we'd write our own guidebook—once we figured everything out, together.

THE BREAKRIVER BANSHEE

BY ABIGAIL MCKENNA

1874 - Arizona Territory

Otis Johnston was dead. Zeke knew it the minute he ducked through the door of the haphazard shack at the edge of town. There wasn't a smell, exactly. More like a feeling. The whole place felt stiff, like it had stopped breathing when its owner had. It made everything in him want to turn around and walk out. But his boots kept shuffling forward, into the small space.

Sure enough, there was Otis, on a cot in the corner. If his skin hadn't had a blue tint to it, he might've been sleeping. Zeke removed his hat respectfully and turned to address his father outside.

"You might want to talk to Mr. Dyer. I don't think Otis is coming in today."

The sheriff didn't say a word, just stepped aside and let Doc Williams in first. The town doctor was a portly, middle-aged man with dark skin, graying hair, and spectacles. He shooed Zeke out of the way so he could examine the corpse. Sheriff Taylor pulled away from the doorway to search the perimeter. After a few moments, the doctor squinted up at Zeke.

"I'll have to get the body out of here before I can really tell what happened, but something about it seems strange."

"What kind of strange?"

"I know folks can just keel over, but Otis was healthy as an ox. Never got drunk a day in his life. But there are no bullets. No strangulation marks." His voice was rough from the allergies that always plagued him this time of year.

"Can't think of anyone who'd want ol' Otis dead," Zeke offered, rubbing his fingers along the brim of his hat.

"Just what I was thinkin'. Strange." The doctor went back to his examination.

Slowly, methodically, Zeke turned in a circle, taking in everything there was to see about the tiny shack. Not that there was much to see. Otis had spent most of his time either in the mine or the saloon. This place was really only used for sleeping, which was evident by the fact that the only piece of furniture other than the bed was a rickety table piled with Otis's mining equipment. Three pegs on the far wall held a threadbare coat and an extra shirt. A thin layer of sand and dust covered it all, one of the dangers of living in Breakriver.

In the almost 30 years he'd worked the mine, Otis hadn't missed a shift, not even when he was ill. It was this odd turn of events that had led Dyer, the manager of the copper mine, to ask the Sheriff to check in on him. They'd grabbed Doc on the way, on Zeke's instinct that something was wrong. He'd never hated being right until today.

As Zeke finished his visual scan of the room, the Sheriff

returned to the doorway, jerking his head to signal for Zeke to join him.

"What're you thinking, Pop?"

Sheriff Taylor grunted, and Zeke fell in step beside him to stride around the shack. A fire pit had been assembled out back, a circle of stones with a cast iron pot hanging from a stake beside it. It looked like it belonged on the open prairie.

"Found this in the ashes." He passed Zeke a charred scrap of paper, perhaps the remains of a paycheck. Zeke turned it over; two words were scrawled on the back in a shaky hand - *ALIVE* and the letters *CLEM*. The rest of the second word had burned away. "Someone didn't want this to be found."

"So you think it could be murder?" Zeke murmured, handing back the paper.

"Didn't say that." The Sheriff squinted at the scrap and scratched the back of his neck. "Just find it kinda suspicious, that's all."

"Should I ask Annie to take a look?"

"Why not?" His father shrugged. "She has a good eye for catching things we don't."

Running his fingers through his dark blond hair, Zeke put his hat back on and pulled a small leather notebook out of his pocket and started sketching out a visual of the burned note. Annie would probably make fun of him for clue-collecting, but he liked keeping his thoughts orderly.

There wasn't a reason, really, to think anything sinister was afoot. But something about it felt wrong, and he didn't like it.

ZEKE FOUND Annabelle O'Malley where he always found her, with her hands buried in the soil of her garden. Her eyes were closed as she knelt with her head bowed, almost like she was praying. She breathed slowly, letting the magic seep from her hands and into the soil. From Zeke's under-standing, green users like Annie could bend the earth to their whims, encouraging life where there otherwise might be none. Different users had different specialties, depending on their color of choice. They could convince any color to help if they tried, though - the cabinet of various colors of liquified magic in the O'Malley kitchen stood testament to that fact.

Annie's happy place was her garden, he knew that. She'd spent hours in the space behind the hotel she helped her mother run, coaxing it to life. Zeke had always loved to join her there. Any plant he was given sole custody over was often dead before he could blink, though, no matter how many times Annie told him exactly what to do. But under her care, and with her green magic, the garden was lush and vibrant. It had always been safe. He hated having to bring such terrible news into it. His approach was quiet, to avoid startling her.

After a moment that seemed like a long time, Annie sat back, rolling her shoulders with a contented sigh. She turned to him and grinned, and he told himself he didn't notice how her red hair shimmered in the sunlight, or that the grin made the freckles on her face dance. It didn't work.

"Hey, Zeke."

"Hey." He forced his mouth into half of a smile.

She pushed up to stand, wiped her hands off on her apron. Studied him. He tried to hold her gaze but couldn't do it.

"What happened?"

He never had been able to keep secrets from her.

"Otis Johnston is dead. Gone in his sleep, we think."

A little knot formed between her eyebrows as she absorbed the information.

"Did Doc look at him?"

"Yeah... he's gotta look closer. It doesn't seem to be murder."

Annie laughed dryly. "That's good, I guess." She picked up her basket and wrinkled her nose up at him. "You don't sound sure." There was a time when they had been the same height - she had been one of the first to look him square in the eye when they met ten years ago. Now her head barely cleared his shoulder when they stood side by side. Or it would, if he would do as Mrs. O'Malley commanded and quit slouching.

He fell in step beside her as she walked the short distance to the hotel's back door. Shoving his hands into his pockets, his fingers found his notebook. The mysterious letters flashed into his mind.

"I'd feel better if you take a look."

She nodded.

"I'm happy to help any way I can. Come inside first, though. Mama will want to see you."

"I won't tell her about Otis yet."

"Probably for the best."

Zeke held the back door open so she could pass

through into the kitchen. Jenny Haggerty, a miner's wife who took shifts cooking at the hotel, was pulling a pan of biscuits from the oven. Before she could make a move to stop him, Zeke had snatched one from the pan and tossed it back and forth between his hands so it wouldn't burn him.

"Ezekiel Taylor!" Jenny hollered, swatting at him with her dishtowel. "Those are for the guests and you know it!"

He stuck the piping hot biscuit in his mouth and sped to put the table between them. She came after him, not quite hiding the laughter she was trying to keep down. Annie ignored their antics and started unpacking her basket of fresh vegetables onto the countertop.

"What in heaven's name is going on in here?" Charlotte O'Malley blew in like a wind and put a hand out to catch Zeke's arm as he passed by her. Thus stopped, Jenny caught him quickly and kept up her dishtowel attack.

"This one stole a biscuit straight from the pan like some kind of hoodlum." Now she couldn't hold back the laughter, and it burst from her like a song. Zeke had to laugh along, even as he raised his arm as a shield against her fearsome towel. It felt good to laugh.

Charlotte gave his shoulder one gentle swat for good measure before giving a chuckle of her own.

"Well I suppose the guests won't want it now, will they, Deputy Taylor?"

"No, ma'am." He removed his hat, flushing at the official title as Jenny relented and went back to her work. Mrs. O'Malley tucked a few stray hairs behind her ears, dark brown but otherwise very much like her daughter's.

"Since you're here, could you give me a hand with one

of the doors upstairs? It's still squeaking something awful." Charlotte's voice was slow and soft like silk, leftover from her former life as a southern belle.

Before Zeke could answer her question, Annie jumped in.

"He'll have to come back later, Mama. The Sheriff needed my help with something at the office."

Her mother clicked her tongue in disappointment but let Annie drag him out the back again.

"I'll check it out tomorrow, Mrs. O'Malley," Zeke called over his shoulder, and she smiled as she waved them on. Annie shook her head as they started down the main road towards Otis's shack.

"You can't deny her anything, can you?"

"I learned a long time ago never to say no to an O'Malley woman." He sent her an impish wink and she rolled her eyes.

"Did you burn your hands?" Digging into the canvas satchel at her side, she held up a small glass bottle of bright yellow liquid - healing magic. He chuckled.

"No, but thank you for the offer."

Annie shrugged and put the bottle away, then handed him a biscuit with slices of tomato and cucumber inside. He stared at it for a second. She gave a knowing smirk.

"Figured you'd forgotten to eat anything, after finding Otis and all." She patted her satchel again. "I brought one for your dad, too."

"What would I do without you?"

She laughed, one of his favorite sounds in the world.

"Let's hope we never have to find out, eh?"

He grinned and started eating. A life without Annie in it wasn't any life he wanted.

———

"I DIDN'T REALIZE Otis lived like this." Annie wrinkled her nose and surveyed the dilapidated shack, turning in a slow circle similar to his earlier.

"A lot of the miners do." Zeke propped his hat back on his head, trying to view the scene with fresh eyes. "The ones without families, anyway."

"It's sad, to think of him being alone when he went."

"Well, the question of whether or not he had company at the end is exactly what we're trying to figure out, right?"

"Fair enough." Annie picked up the burnt scrap of paper from where they'd left it on the table earlier and rubbed her thumb across the strange letters. "*CLEM*? Not too many words start with clem."

"That's what I thought." He grabbed his notebook from his pocket and flipped it open. "No incriminating marks on the corpse, no sign of suspicious activity outside. Pop is out interviewing the neighbors to see if they heard anything."

Annie had started twisting the curly end of her braid around her finger. "And he was laid out like he was sleeping?"

"I thought so. He seemed pretty peaceful."

"Hmm." She chewed on her lip. "Any chance he just went in the night?"

"A good chance, probably. Murder seems odd for this town. Pop and Doc both agreed."

"So do I, for what it's worth. It's just those letters that make me wonder." She looked at him, but more like she was looking through him. "Clemency. Clematis, that's a flower. Clemton isn't far from here." She shifted her gaze back to the table, and her next word was almost whispered. "Clementine."

"Clementine?"

"Yeah…" Her brow furrowed as she called forth memories. "We had some folks who stayed at the hotel a while back and said they'd heard a story of a family in town who died thirty years ago in a freak accident. The daughter's name was Clementine. It stuck with me for some reason."

Zeke raised an eyebrow.

"Think that has anything to do with this?"

"Maybe not, but I'd bet a girl who was killed here has more to do with Otis's death than the clematis flower does." She lifted a shoulder. "But maybe that's just me."

"Fair enough," Zeke echoed, jotting down the name in his notes. "I'll see if anyone knows anything about what happened to her."

"Any ideas in there as to why Otis would write only part of a word onto this paper?" Annie jutted her chin jokingly in the direction of his notebook. He shut it with a snap.

"Hard to know when we don't know what the rest of the word is. We don't even know if Otis was the one to write it."

"Could've been the killer, I guess." Annie tossed her braid over her shoulder. "Could have nothing to do with his death at all."

The door to the shack moved and they both jumped. Zeke's father entered, his hand on the gun holstered on his hip. Samuel Taylor was an intimidating man when he wanted to be, broad-shouldered and tall. For most of his life, Zeke had been told he was his spitting image, but his father had a confidence that he never thought he'd gain.

"I heard voices. Glad to see it's you." He nodded at them. "How you doin', Annie?"

"Been better, Sheriff." Annie tilted her head toward the empty bed, then rifled through her bag and handed him a sandwich. "Thought y'all might need a pick-me-up."

Sheriff Taylor didn't hesitate to take a giant bite, then chuckled.

"Son, when're you gonna ask this girl to marry you so we can keep her around for a good long time?"

"Pop!" Zeke ducked his head so the brim of his hat would hide the reddening of his face, but he could hear Annie's soft giggle.

"Did you find anything out from the neighbors, Sheriff?" Annie had always been good at deflecting conversations she knew he'd hate.

"Not too much. Nobody heard any sounds of a struggle, which lines up with the lack of any evidence of one. A couple people said they thought they heard someone cryin' far off in the distance, but most of them figured it was the wind."

"Crying?" Annie's brow creased again. "That's interesting."

"Interesting how?" Zeke raised his head in curiosity.

Annie cast a quick glance around the shack. "Is there anything else you need me for here?"

The abruptness of her tone made him pause. "No, I guess not."

"Okay. Good to see you, Sheriff."

"Always a pleasure, Annie."

She pushed past them and out of the shack. Zeke and his father exchanged a confused glance before Zeke followed her.

"Annie?" He almost had to jog to catch up with her. "Annie, stop, what happened?"

She put up a hand, the other tugging at her braid. "Hang on, Zeke, I'm thinking." She kept walking, slower than before. He waited, keeping her pace but letting her think, trying to calm his own heart from running with worry.

"Maybe I can help talk this out, Annie."

"Crying, Zeke. People heard crying from a long way away, and I'd venture to guess they heard some singing too."

"Well, like Pop said, it was probably the wind."

"But it could have been something else." She was breathless. "Something worse. So much worse."

"You have an idea what that could be?"

"Yeah." Her eyes met his, and the unsettled look in them startled him. "But if it is what I think it might be... we'd better pray I'm wrong."

JEREMIAH O'MALLEY'S office had been condensed down to one corner of the hotel's parlor, the books kept in a glass case and the desk offered to guests who needed a place to write correspondence. A talented magic user in his own right, he'd taught his daughter everything she knew, most of it posthumously as she pored over his writings and books. But even now, almost eight years after the man's death, a feeling of him lingered on the furniture.

As Annie flung open the case and started shuffling through the large leather-bound books inside, Zeke couldn't help but wish Mr. O'Malley was still around. Maybe he'd know what to do about this thing, whatever it was. Or at least he'd know how to calm his daughter.

Annie hoisted a thick book onto the desk and started combing through the table of contents. Zeke could only watch, slightly concerned, as she flipped to a page near the end and started reading it to herself. After a moment, she straightened and sighed.

"Corrupted. I was hoping it wouldn't be a Corrupted."

"A what now?"

She pointed at a paragraph in the tome; Zeke leaned over to peer at it.

"When a magic user abuses magic and purposefully takes too much of it with malicious intent, red magic, chaos magic, can take over," Annie explained. "It corrupts the user, turns them into something…else. Vampire, wolvin, siren, banshee, something like that."

"And these…things. Are they dangerous?"

"Very. Usually. Most of them were murderers or thieves before they were corrupted, so once they've got extra power…it usually doesn't go well."

Zeke scratched the back of his neck.

"So you think we've got one of these things roaming around and killing folks?"

"I'm still hoping Otis just went in his sleep." She hugged herself, and he wished he could wrap his arms around her. "No marks on the body, so that rules out a vampire. A wolvin would've been more violent, and Otis was in his bed, so it probably wasn't a siren either. That leaves a banshee."

"What does a banshee do?"

"They cry. They mourn for their victims before they kill them." Annie's lips pulled into a thin line. "They siphon a person's spirit - remove it from the body before its time."

A chill ran down Zeke's spine.

"So let's say this is a banshee that we're dealing with." Zeke's tone was quiet. "How do we stop it?"

Annie sat in the desk chair heavily, propping her chin on her hand as she went back to reading.

"I'm not sure. There's not as much known about them as the others." She sighed again. "According to this, you're lucky to kill them before they kill you."

Zeke's hand drifted to the holster on his hip. "So, what, we just have to wait and see if it strikes again?"

"I guess so." She sat back. "If we knew who they used to be, before they were corrupted, maybe we could figure out where they've holed up."

"Okay. I'll add red magic users to my question list. Surely someone would remember if there was a user powerful enough to get corrupted, right?"

"You'd think so." Annie pressed her fingers against her forehead, then stretched her shoulders, and he could practically see her put her fear aside. "I've gotta go help Mama, we're starting on the laundry today."

"Annie." She looked up at him. "Thank you." Her feeble smile warmed him. "Pop and I will handle this, okay? It's gonna be fine."

She caught his hand as he turned to go.

"Just promise me you'll be careful. Don't go after this thing alone."

"I promise."

HIS MOTHER HAD BEEN in his dreams again. Caught under the crushed stagecoach, bandits around her, reaching out her hands to him, crying, helpless. His feet were sinking in the ground, keeping him from reaching her, even while he screamed her name.

He couldn't save her. He was useless. He was alone.

Zeke rubbed his hands over his face to try and stop them from shaking. It wasn't the first time he'd had the nightmare, and it probably wouldn't be the last. But that didn't change the way it clawed his heart open. It had been two years since she died; two long years of helping his father hunt down every one of the bandits that had circled the town like vultures, the ones who had found prey in his mother. He wasn't sure he recognized the boy he'd been then.

He sat up and swung his legs over the side of the bed. A walk was usually the only thing to clear his mind. Slipping on his pants and boots, he tiptoed his way downstairs and out the front door, avoiding the squeaky floorboards in an attempt to let his father sleep.

The sky had a grayish tint - sunrise wasn't far away. Shoving his hands in his pockets against the early morning chill, Zeke meandered his way in a loop around the Sheriff's station. Trying to dispel a memory he hadn't even experienced. All he wanted to do was go talk to Annie, but the light in her window was off and he didn't want to wake her.

They'd been unsuccessful in trying to find any more information about Otis's death the day before. Doc still hadn't settled on a cause of death. Zeke hated not being able to move forward, feeling the trail go cold. If there even was a trail to follow.

He scuffed his boot into the dirt. Potential murder wasn't in his area of expertise.

A voice singing in the distance caused his head to snap up in the direction of the mountains. It was low, female, if he had to guess, her song mournful and slow. He couldn't make out the words, but it made him want to cry. It sounded like his mother.

"Oh, I'm losing it." He scrubbed his hands over his face again, turning back to the house, and jumped. A girl stood between him and the door, about Annie's height, with red hair almost as wild as his friend's. She was startlingly like Annie, actually. But her eyes were what he couldn't look away from. Wider than they should have been, rimmed red around the edges, dark and haunted.

"Can I…help you, miss?" He hadn't noticed how hoarse he sounded. The girl regarded him, unblinking. It made him shiver in spite of himself. Her skin was as pale as her dress in the early light.

"You're the Sheriff's boy."

It wasn't a question. Her words were rough, thick with emotion, but somehow cold.

"Yes, I am."

"No, you can't help me." Her eyes dropped for a moment. "No one can."

"I'm sorry." He didn't know what else to say. A tiny smile lifted her lips, but she turned away to start walking down the packed dirt street.

"Wait, miss?"

She paused.

"Who are you?" He had to ask.

A deep breath raised her shoulders.

"I'm nobody."

It was Jenny Haggerty this time. Zeke had barely gotten back to sleep after his strange meeting before he was shuffling up behind his father, rubbing the sandpaper feeling out of his eyes to squint at Doc Williams through the open door.

"I hate to wake y'all so early, but I thought you might need to come along."

Seth Haggerty was a man nearing middle-age, meaning his days in the mine were probably numbered, but he never let that stop him. He'd always had a laugh larger than life, served the role of deacon diligently at the church. But now as he stood next to the doctor, he seemed old, his shoulders hunched forward and his eyes glazed over. From his expression of shock and anger, he hadn't quite absorbed the information.

The Sheriff grabbed his hat off the rack. "Seth, why don't you head across the street with Zeke and see if the O'Malley ladies have some coffee brewing? Doc and I will take a look around."

Zeke wanted to protest, but Seth's hands had started to tremble.

"Come on, Mr. Haggerty, I'm sure Mrs. O'Malley will have a good breakfast for you."

Zeke guided the man out of the Sheriff's station gently.

Annie answered his knock on the back door, her hair loose around her shoulders as she pulled a dressing gown around her. Maybe it was because he was tired, maybe it was because she looked pretty, but all his brain could muster was,

"Hey."

"Hey yourself." She gave him a smile and glanced at Seth. "Good morning, Mr. Haggerty."

"Mornin', Annie…" The man seemed to wilt before them. Zeke put an arm around his shoulders and cleared his throat.

"Is your mama up? I'm afraid we've got some bad news."

Annie's lips pressed together as she nodded.

"I'll put some coffee on. Come on in."

Within five minutes, Charlotte sat at the kitchen table with Seth, her hand patting his arm as he mumbled breathlessly about everything that had occurred prior to his stop at the Sheriff's station. Annie passed cups of coffee around, then started preparing some eggs. Every so often, she would sniff or wipe tears from her eyes with the back of her hand; each time, Zeke felt his heart squeeze tighter. Without a word, he passed her his handkerchief. She accepted it with a small smile and scooped some of the eggs onto a plate.

"I'm not hungry," Seth said softly, shrinking further into himself.

"You have to keep your strength up," Charlotte's tone didn't leave room for argument, and when Annie slid the plate over, she watched him sternly until he ate. She would mourn later, in her own time; Seth was her priority now.

Annie stood next to Zeke, who was leaning against the counter and staring into his coffee.

"Strange coincidence, huh?" he offered quietly. She gave a little exhale of a laugh, her eyes puffy.

"You don't think it's a coincidence."

"How do you know that?"

"I know you haven't stopped tapping your finger against that mug handle since I gave it to you, which means your brain is working through something."

He frowned, setting down the drink.

"Breakriver lost two people in two days. We haven't had a funeral since…sorry." She stuttered to a stop, but he knew the next words were supposed to be "your mother's". Somehow, it didn't hurt as much as he thought it should.

Zeke shifted his shoulders so that he faced her.

"I need to talk to you."

She glanced at her mother, bit her lip, and dragged him after her into the hallway. Once the parlor door was shut behind them, she snagged one of her curls and started twisting it around her finger. "Did you find out…anything?"

"I had another nightmare."

"Your mother?"

He nodded, the memory of it making his frown deepen. She watched him for a second.

"It's been two years, Zeke. You're allowed to miss her."

"I can't think straight. I don't know what I'm doing. If

there is a pattern here, I can't see it." Zeke sat in the desk chair, taking off his hat and dragging his fingers through his hair. Annie tilted her head down at him, then reached into his jacket pocket and pulled out his notebook before he could react. Pulling up a footstool next to his chair, she opened the notebook on her lap and started writing with the pencil he kept tucked inside.

"What're you doing?" He tugged his jacket tighter around him.

"What you're always suggesting." She angled the page so that he could see. "I'm making a list."

If trying to solve potential murders hadn't made it a ridiculously improper time, Zeke would have asked Annie to marry him right then and there.

"We know Otis died sometime in the night, and he was found by you and your father when he didn't show up to work, right?"

Zeke nodded once.

"Seth said Jenny also died sometime in the night, and he found her this morning."

"Yep."

"Seth didn't mention anything about any odd markings on her body, and Otis didn't have any of those either." Annie tapped the pencil against her lips. "So either they both had a heart attack, and it all just is happenstance, or…"

"We should pursue that banshee angle."

"You think so?" She went very still.

"Call it a hunch." He leaned forward to take the note-book. Her list looked nothing like his would have, and the handwriting went crooked halfway across the page like the letters wanted to fly away. He also knew he'd never tear this page out, if he could help it.

"Any ideas on where to start?" She stood, her feet shifting like they wanted a purpose.

"I was thinking the church. Death records, that kind of thing. If we've got a banshee around here, surely it's struck before."

"Good thought." She bobbed her head once, then turned to the parlor door. "Let me get dressed."

"You don't have to come with me if you don't want to."

"Are you kidding?" She gave him a grin as crooked as her letters. "Research is my middle name." With a toss of her head, she flounced out of the room, and he did his best to stifle a snicker before calling after her,

"I thought it was Caroline!"

———

Pastor Long didn't quite understand what they were looking for.

"You want to know if there were ever any suspicious deaths here?"

"In the past thirty years or so, yes," Zeke affirmed, his hat tucked under his arm as they stood in front of the little church. The pastor rubbed his bearded chin and frowned.

"Well, I'm not sure, Deputy. We don't have many records, but why don't we walk and see what my old memory scrounges up?" Alan Long was barely fifty and happily single, as much a staple of the community as the clapboard building he maintained.

Annie had made a beeline for the cemetery beside the

church, and now Zeke and the pastor strolled after her. She was peering at various headstones, her fingers trailing over them as she moved.

"What exactly are we looking for?" Zeke asked her under his breath.

"I'm not sure." She squinted at a particularly worn stone. "I've just got a feeling." They wandered together through the small graveyard. Pastor Long pointed out particularly interesting lives. Breakriver as a town had only been around for fifty years or so and had been blessed not to lose too many citizens in that time, but their cemetery had the usual infant-sized headstones, a few elderly folks who'd passed on peacefully. Annie's father. Zeke's mother. Soon, Otis and Jenny would be added to its number.

"Aha!" Annie's exclamation broke Zeke from his thoughts. She squatted beside three headstones that had been tucked back in the corner of the fencing. He caught up with her and leaned down to study them. Three names - Stanley Hodges, Norman Sheppard, and Clementine Sheppard.

"Clementine!" Zeke said, pointing at the name. Annie brushed some dirt off the marker and read,

"Clementine Sheppard - September 8 1826 to September 12 1849; gone but not forgotten." She sat back on her heels. "She was twenty-three. Same as us." A chill gripped the back of his neck despite the sun beating down on them. He knelt beside Annie.

"This isn't much help in figuring out what happened to her."

"Now that is a sad story." Pastor Long had come up behind them, startling Zeke so that he almost toppled over.

Annie, unaffected, stood to talk with him, and Zeke scrambled to his feet after her.

"What kind of tragedy?"

"There was a flash flood in and around the mine across the river. This was just after I came to town, as a matter of fact. The Sheppard family and Hodges were caught in it, God rest their souls. There were plenty of folks at the funeral, though most were there for Norman and Clementine. Hodges was…" He considered his words. "Not a town favorite. Had a tendency toward gambling with other people's money." He chortled. "Well, look at me, speaking ill of the dead. I really didn't know any of them that well. Still, it was a tragedy, pure and simple. Is that what you meant by suspicious?"

"Maybe, Pastor." Annie sent Zeke a sideways glance. "Thank you for all of your help."

"Any time, of course. Have a blessed day." He shook hands with Zeke and politely nodded to Annie, and the two left the churchyard. Zeke could practically see gears turning in Annie's head as they walked toward the Haggerty house.

"You have an idea."

"Half of one, anyway." She stuck her hands in the pockets of her sweater. "I was just wondering if Clementine Sheppard isn't in that grave."

Zeke's even gait stalled.

"How do you mean?"

Annie raised her shoulders.

"Twenty-five years isn't a long time, really. She could still be out there somewhere."

"You don't think…" Zeke swallowed. "You don't think

she could be the banshee, do you?" The light around them seemed to dim a little, as if even the sun was a bit afraid of the conversation. "Maybe the accident wasn't such an accident."

"We'd have to find her to know for sure, and we don't want to do that." The flicker of hollow fear that flashed across Annie's face struck him. He'd seen the same expression on the mystery girl last night. That thought led him to the next one - he'd seen her. Clementine. It had to be.

He could have stopped her. Jenny might still be alive right now.

He was useless. Again.

"Zeke?"

He blinked out of his mental spiral to see Annie watching him carefully.

"Are you okay?"

"Yeah. Yeah, I'm fine."

She didn't look convinced. He started walking again, pulling his hat low across his forehead. He had an idea, and he had a feeling she wouldn't like it.

WHEN BREAKRIVER WENT to sleep that night, Zeke's haphazard plan went into motion. He'd laid it out in his notebook in neatly lettered thoughts.

Find Clementine. (Cemetery? Will she find me?)

Ask her to stop killing folks. (If she won't, arrest her.)

He didn't have many plans beyond that. Something in her eyes the night they'd spoken made him think she might listen to reason. He could be wrong. But he wasn't going to let anyone else die if he had the chance to save them.

With an unlit lantern in one hand, matches in his jacket pocket, and his pistol holstered on his hip, just in case, he slipped quietly out of the house. The sky was clear, moonlight washing the town in silver. It was a beautiful night to chase a monster.

The graveyard seemed like a logical place to start, so he made his way there, leaving the lantern dark. No point in announcing his presence to anyone who didn't need to know. The walk was uneventful, though his mind was racing, rehearsing what he would say when he saw her again.

What does one say to a person who was supposed to have died years ago, only to return and potentially kill two people?

Like silent soldiers, the headstones stood watch as he approached the cemetery, his step as cautious and quiet as possible. Not that he believed in ghosts.

"Although," he muttered, "we're dealing with a banshee, so who knows anything anymore?" With a sigh, he started toward Clementine's grave. Before he'd made it halfway there, he heard two things: footsteps in the gravel behind him and singing in the far distance. On instinct, his hand went to his gun holster as he turned.

"What the heck do you think you're doing?" Annie's voice, edged with frustration and something else. Panic? She stared up at him in the moonlight, an unlit lantern, much like his, in one hand and the other on her hip. His brain was too startled to come up with a good lie.

"Waiting for Clementine." Instantly he regretted the words as Annie went very still.

"Zeke, you promised me you wouldn't go after this thing alone."

"Well, what are you doing here?" He tried to change the trajectory, but she wasn't fooled.

"Following my best friend who just snuck out of his own house and trying to keep him from doing something incredibly stupid."

"Annie, I'm not trying to fight her, I'm just trying to talk to her."

"You can't reason with a banshee! We've already talked about that!" Her whispered shouts felt like needles pricking his skin. In all the years they'd known each other, he wasn't sure he'd actually seen her angry. But she was furious now, the kind of anger that made her whole body stiff and tears form in her eyes. He hated it; hated that he'd done it to her. She took a deep breath, though it stuttered in the middle.

"Are you planning on ending this?" Her words were tight. He hesitated before nodding. She breathed again, letting her gaze shift past him towards the mountains, the mine, and the singing. "My guess for her hideout is the old mine. If her overuse of magic is what caused the flood, it was probably the site of her corruption too. She might still be there."

"That's…exactly what I was thinking," Zeke lied as he shifted his weight, unsure of what the next step should be.

"We should go home and investigate in the morning," Annie offered, reading his mind as usual.

"No. Someone else could be dead by morning, I'm going now." He marched past her before he could change his mind. "You go home."

"If you think I'm gonna let you go after this thing by yourself, Ezekiel Taylor, you're crazy."

"That's not a suggestion, Annabelle O'Malley. Go home."

"And I'm not asking for your permission, I'm informing you that I'm coming along."

"That's not an option." He tried again to walk away.

"We take care of each other."

He stopped.

"That's what we said all those years ago, you remember that?" Her tone was sharp, testing him. He remembered.

They'd been fifteen, a week after her father died. His mother had dragged him to the funeral in his Sunday best to comfort the widow. Preferring the silence of the cemetery to the tears inside, Zeke had taken the first chance to slip outside, only to find that he wasn't alone.

The redheaded girl in the black dress, watching the deep hole in the ground with a somber, thoughtful look on her face; his brain didn't have time to catch up before his feet were moving in her direction. She hadn't looked up at his approach but had simply said in a flat voice, "We don't have anyone to protect us now, Mama and me."

"I'll take care of you." What had possessed him to say it, he still didn't know. It just felt right, and he'd meant it. The tiny smile that slipped onto her face confirmed it in his soul.

"We'll take care of each other."

They'd been inseparable ever since.

He turned back to her. Her eyes were burning.

"I intend to keep my half of the bargain." She put a hand on her hip. "Plus, if you don't let me come with you, I'm going straight to your father to tell him your hair-brained scheme. It's up to you." The arch of her eyebrows told him that she knew she had won. He tried one last time.

"You're a green magic user, what exactly are you going to do against a banshee?"

"Same as you, I expect." She bent down and, to his surprise, retrieved a pistol that was strapped to her calf. "I'll shoot it."

The silent headstone soldiers could be his witnesses - Zeke Taylor was in love with Annie O'Malley.

ONE BRIDGE LED where they wanted to go. When it was founded, the town had been on the west side of the river, built up around the silver mine that later flooded. In the twenty-five years since the Sheppard incident, a vein of copper had been found in the hills upriver on the east side, and Breakriver relocated to where it was now.

Zeke vaguely remembered asking his father about the abandoned buildings as a young boy, when they first arrived. He'd been told it was better not to know, one of his father's classic lines for saying he wasn't sure.

Passing by the abandoned shells of what had once been the town sent a chill through Zeke's bones. Annie had lit the lanterns, though they kept them low, trying to avoid catching the attention of anyone on the other shore. The light did little to keep the shadows at bay but kept them from twisting their ankles as they walked.

About twenty minutes passed, enough time for Zeke's mind to run through every terrible thing that could be hiding in the dark buildings, before they reached the entrance to the old mine. Wooden planks had been nailed across the tunnel opening at some point but had been hacked away, leaving splinters scattered in the dirt.

"Correct me if I'm wrong," Annie whispered, "but that looks as if it was opened from the inside, does it not?"

Another unwelcome shiver went through Zeke's body.

"It looks like a crypt."

"Agreed," Annie grimaced. "We're going in, though...right?"

Zeke sighed, gripped his pistol, and slipped inside. Shadows swallowed him as if he'd stepped down the throat of a dragon or some other creature of legend. He lifted his lantern to illuminate the gentle downward slope of the ground, a track bolted to it with a dusty and rusty train to transport miners. With a soft squeak that she tried to hide, Annie followed him in. They approached the little train and Annie dug through her pockets. "Aha, see, I knew you'd be glad you brought me along." She held up a glass bottle of magic with a flourish, its orange glow reflected in her eyes.

"You just happen to have a bottle of orange magic with you?"

"I'm a woman of mystery." She tossed her braid. "That and Papa always said when one lives in a mining town, it's best to keep orange magic in your pocket."

"Can't argue with that."

Annie examined the transport train, stopping to pour a bit of liquid magic into the small engine, then coaxing it to give the wheels forward motion. With a screech of protest at their disuse, the wheels turned once, and Annie jumped on.

"Shall we have an adventure?" She asked, trying to make her tone teasing.

"Are you sure this thing is safe?" Zeke regarded the machine dubiously.

"Nope. Hence the adventure." Between the lanterns and the orange magic, her eyes sparkled now.

"You seem awfully chipper about this."

"Well, it's either laugh or cry, right?"

With a shake of his head, Zeke sat beside her, and she urged the magic to take them deeper into the mine. The darkness grew as the walls closed in around them. Annie reached over and gripped his hand.

After a few moments that felt like forever, the walls widened again, and the train burst into what was almost open air. The two shared a confused glance, lifting their lanterns higher.

"Whoa," Zeke breathed. To the right of the tracks, the ground dropped away into a canyon. Veins of silver ore on the far side caught the light and bounced it back around the room. Zeke glanced down and shut his eyes in an instant. Water rushed far below, lots of it. He had almost forgotten how much he hated heights.

The train started to slow as Annie gaped at their surroundings.

"This is incredible! The accident must have been…*enormous*. It blew a hole in the mountain!"

"It did kill two people." Zeke tried and failed to take the strain out of his words. "Could we please move on?"

"Oh. Sorry." Annie focused again on the magic in the engine and they began moving forward.

Singing, echoing off the rock walls, made them both jump.

"She's here," Zeke said quietly.

"That's why we're here, right?"

"Right." Every bit of the plan he'd made escaped him. This was crazy, and somehow he'd roped the girl he loved into it. Annie nudged his shoulder. She knew him too well.

"You'll know what to do. You always do."

"No, I don't."

"Yes, you do, Zeke." She squeezed his hand. "I know you do."

The train rattled as the ground beside the tracks widened again. Another tunnel opened before them, but Annie slowed their ride before they entered. Zeke looked at her, confused.

"I think it might be coming from down there." She hopped off the train and moved toward the edge of the canyon. "It sounds almost like..." She swung her lantern higher. "I can't see anything. Just a lot of shadows and-"

The rock beneath her crumbled, and she toppled forward. Before Zeke could reach her, she'd fallen over the edge with a scream.

No. No. Not again.

Her scream cut short with a sickening snap, and his heart stopped until he heard her groan.

"Annie?" Her name choked his throat like an invisible hand as panic shot him forward, and he dropped to his knees by the edge.

She was there, on an outcropping of rock maybe ten

feet down, on her back with one leg at a very incorrect angle beneath her. Breathing. Alive. In pain. But alive.

"Hang on, hang on, I'm coming." Zeke looked around wildly, trying to make his brain think logically.

"No!" Annie grunted in pain, her face contorting. "No, Zeke!"

"But you-"

"Need help. We need help."

"Right. Doc. I'll get Doc." He stood, only able to hear the blood rushing in his ears and her stuttering breaths. "I'll get Doc. Stay right there."

Any other day she would have laughed. *"Not like I can go anywhere, Zeke."* She didn't even smile. That was worrying.

Zeke was ready to run back across the tracks. He'd crawl if he had to. But before he could, his ear caught the singing again, closer than before. Coming from the tunnel.

Clementine.

She could kill them; she probably would kill them. But she was closer than Doc, and she had magic. Zeke hesitated for a moment, before hoisting his lantern and running full tilt into the tunnel, his thudding footsteps echoing back at him.

He skidded to a stop at what appeared to be a room carved into the rock wall. There was a table fashioned out of scrap wood, a barrel for a chair, a lit lantern hanging from a metal hook. The banshee, sitting on the barrel and hugging herself, rocking back and forth as she sang her lament. There weren't words that he could make out, just pitiful wailing that was so beautiful it made him ache.

With his scuffling stop at her door, the banshee shot to

her feet and stared at him, tears shining on her face. "You?" The whispered word held shock.

"Clementine, please, I need your help."

She took a step back as if he'd struck her.

"How did you get here? How do you know who I am?"

"Otis's house, he'd written out part of your name."

She shook her head.

"I didn't… I didn't do anything to Otis. Not on purpose. He only wanted to help me."

"I believe you." He did. He didn't know why, but he did. "But please, Clementine. My friend, my Annie, she's hurt bad and I'm not a magic user."

"Neither am I. Not anymore."

"Please." The word stuck in his throat. "I can't… I can't lose her too."

The banshee watched him for a moment, her wide, mournful eyes solemn. Then she tucked her pale arms against her worn dress and took a deep breath.

"Take me to her."

They retraced his steps until they found the spot. Clementine shrank back from the edge but Zeke inched forward until he could see Annie again in the light of his lantern. Her own light had been smashed in the fall, the wreckage littered beside her.

"Annie, I found Clementine. She's going to help."

Annie's eyes widened, but when she tried to talk, she coughed instead. Zeke wheeled on the banshee, who looked smaller than before.

"I can't," she whispered, starting to cry again. "I'm sorry."

"Yes, you can. You have to." He started to reach for her, but she jerked back.

"Don't! Don't touch me!" She was shaking now. "I hurt people. That's my curse. You shouldn't have come here."

He didn't have time for her crisis of conscience, but he didn't have another choice. So he set down his lantern and spread his hands as if she was a scared animal.

"You don't want to hurt us, Clementine. I know that. If you did, we'd already be dead." She fixed him with a frightened gaze but didn't move otherwise. "I don't think you meant to hurt Otis or Jenny, either. Or your father." Zeke cocked his head. "Am I right?"

"I had to kill Stanley." Her eyes, which were already haunted, seemed to see through him to another time. "I *had* to. He tried to…" A tremor went through her body as she stopped herself. "He was a monster, he didn't deserve to live. The red magic made it sound like it would be so easy. But Papa…" With a little sob, her face crumbled. "Papa wasn't supposed to die. But the storm got so big, and I couldn't… I wasn't… I wasn't strong enough."

"I know how that feels." Without his asking for it, his mind supplied memories of the nightmare.

He'd failed his mother. He'd failed Otis and Jenny. But he wouldn't fail now.

He couldn't fail now.

"Clementine, listen to me." Zeke took a step toward her. "I lost my mother. She went to visit her sister and was ambushed on the way back, and I wasn't there because I made the choice that other things were more important. And I've carried that with me for two years now." His voice was hoarse with emotion. He was dredging up things he hadn't known he'd wanted to admit, but now they were pouring out like his heart had sprung a leak. "I know that's nowhere near twenty-five, but I feel the weight too. And for two years I've wished I could just…hear her voice again. One more time. Ask her…so many questions. She was the wisest woman I've ever known." He took another step; she didn't back away. "I remember, one time, I asked her about death. Someone in town had died, I think, but I asked her why God killed the good people. She said, 'Ezekiel, there's always a reason.' I've found that to be true. And if my losing her was what could save you…" He shook his head. "That's enough reason for me."

"You can't be thankful she's dead."

"If I could go back and make different choices, I'd do it in an instant. But I can't. And neither can you." Slowly, carefully, Zeke put a hand on her arm. "I'm tired of trying to carry the darkness. Aren't you?"

Clementine started crying again, and he pulled back, afraid he'd said something wrong.

"I'm so tired." Her confession was quiet, full of relief. He nodded with a soft smile.

"Let me help you carry it."

She reached a shaking hand forward and he took it, tucked it under his arm. She felt like a little bird, thin and delicate, ready to fly at any moment. But she walked forward steadily, leaning on him. They peered down at Annie, who raised her eyebrows. Clementine turned her face up to Zeke's.

"I have an idea." She lowered herself to her knees, pressing her palms flat against the ground. With a rumble and a grating noise that made Zeke flinch, the stone shifted. Clementine took a quick inhale of delight, then scooted forward and swung her legs over the edge. Zeke almost reached to grab her, but she climbed down calm as anything. She had carved a ladder into the mountain. It explained how she'd made the canyon. Zeke scrambled down after her, rushing to Annie's side. Her skin was almost as pale as Clementine's, but she gripped his hand like a vice as she watched the banshee.

"Green user, huh?" Annie asked.

"I was." A ghost of a smile flitted across Clementine's face.

"Me too." Annie's voice hitched and she let out a little groan.

"Here." Clementine reached into her pocket and gripped a small vial, no bigger than her finger, that glowed a dull yellow.

"You've had yellow magic this whole time?" Zeke asked quietly, trying to keep the smidge of frustration he felt out of his words. Clementine fixed him with her unnervingly wide gaze.

"I wasn't sure it would listen to me anymore." She uncapped the vial and held it up to Annie. "But you're welcome to try."

With a bit of struggle, Annie swallowed the magic, then lay still, her eyes shut in concentration as she encouraged the healing through her body. Zeke brushed the hair from her forehead, wishing he could help. After a minute that felt much longer with his heart lodged in his throat, she breathed easier, and so did he.

"That's better," she gasped; Zeke braced her as she sat

up, and she straightened her legs out in front of her with a sigh. Then she studied Clementine.

"Thank you."

"Yes," Zeke spoke up. "Thank you, Clementine."

The banshee gained that ghost of a smile again.

"It's been a long time since anyone has called me by name. A longer time since I've felt so light." She ducked her head, her wild red curls covering her eyes. "Thank you."

"You could come back with us…if you wanted." Zeke offered as he stood and helped Annie to her feet. It would take her a few days to be back to full strength, but she would live, and for that, he would forever be grateful. Clementine stood as well, hugging her arms around herself again.

"I've hidden in this mountain for all these years." She shrugged. "I wouldn't know how to be around people." She reached up and tugged at one of her curls, and the movement was so like Annie that it caught him off guard for a second.

"Please come," Annie said softly, leaning against Zeke.

"If only to pay your respects to Otis," Zeke added.

"He was dead when I got there, I swear." That frightened animal look appeared for an instant.

"You said he wanted to help you? What did you mean by that?" Zeke couldn't help asking.

"I remembered him from the old days, so I went to see him, a month or so ago, now. He was surprised, but he took pity on me, I suppose. He agreed to do some research for me. But when I went back, he was dead." A tear slid down her cheek. "I still don't know what I am, really."

"I'll help you. We can figure it out." Annie smiled, even

while she swayed a little, and Zeke put his arm around her waist to keep her upright.

"We're happy to have you, if you want. But we need to get Annie home." Zeke started moving, ushering her to the ladder. She was shaking when she reached the top. They boarded the transport train, and Annie gave Clementine the bottle of orange magic, which had somehow avoided being broken in her fall. Slowly, the banshee put a hand on the engine, and after a moment where they all held their breath, it started chugging to the mine entrance. A brightness came to Clementine's face when the magic responded.

Annie slumped against Zeke. He tucked her under his arm and held her close. The sounds of the rushing water faded into the thick silence of the tunnel.

"Annie?" Zeke murmured.

"Hmm?"

"Will you marry me?"

She lifted her head from his shoulder.

"You're asking me while we're inside a mountain where I almost died?"

He flushed.

"I didn't... I mean, I could ask you again later, if you'd rather-"

"Yes." She rested her head on his shoulder again. "Yes, I'll marry you. I've been waiting for you to ask." He had to laugh at that.

"You and half the town."

"That's true." Her giggle made his heart skip a beat. He wished he could bottle the sound - keep it in his pocket like magic and drink it when he needed it.

Sunlight from the mine entrance caught his eye as

Clementine slowed them to a stop. Morning. A new chance. A new start. He breathed in deep, and a weight he hadn't realized he carried released as his neck relaxed.

Zeke led Annie to the entrance, but Clementine hesitated.

"I'll...think about it." She offered them a shaky smile. "Would that be okay?"

"Of course." Zeke reached out a hand and she took it slowly. "We'll be here when you're ready."

She nodded, and they left her there. She would come, he believed that. And when she did, he had no doubt that Mrs. O'Malley would take her in and help her through. They all would.

Doc Williams was the first person they encountered once they got back into town. He took one look at Annie and whisked them off to his office. Once he'd settled Annie on a cushioned sofa with her feet propped up, Zeke recounted where they'd been.

"Goodness, the poor child," the doctor shook his head. "I'm glad you could help each other. Oh, that reminds me." He shuffled through some papers on his desk and handed Zeke a few. "My official ruling on Otis and Jenny - heart failure for him, stroke for her."

"Well, fancy that." He couldn't keep the relief out of his tone. In a way, he was thankful. They'd both gone peacefully.

"So it was all coincidence," Annie noted.

"Maybe," the doctor grinned. "On the other hand, could be something more divine. Maybe somebody needed to get hold of the girl." He went into the back room and left them alone. Zeke dragged over a wooden chair and sat next to Annie.

"Well?" She reached for his hand and entwined their fingers. "There's one thing I'm happy about."

"Just one?" he teased.

"Mhmm. I was right all along. The clematis flower had absolutely nothing to do with any of it." She looked so pleased with herself that he wanted to kiss her. But he settled for a chuckle instead.

He had the rest of their lives to show her how he felt. For today, he would just sit beside her.

NAMAKAOKAHAI'S TREASURE

BY MARIELLA TAYLOR

A great river crashes through the forest, its mighty hands tearing stone and limb. And it was this mighty river that my mother cast me into as a baby. She shrieked up into the canopy, her scream drowning in the cacophony of the waters she hoped would break me. Too small, she cried, too empty, too hollow. Not enough room for fire. The son of Mahuika, the goddess of fire, is nothing without fire. But the river drowned out her cries that day. It pulled me beneath its currents and whispered unto me a name. "Kai," it beckoned me, cradling me in icy fingers, and suddenly, I was no longer empty.

Namakaokahai, the Great River, raised me along her shores. I drank with the brocket, feasted with the jaguars, rested upon the muddy banks with the great serpents, all of us entwined beside the Great River's swollen belly. When I entered her banks, she swept me beneath her great arms and sang to me the song of kinship. And when my timid lungs expelled her love, she guided me back to shore with

smiles and kisses and "Kekahi la e ho'omaka hou"—
Another day to rise again.

And this is how I grew, Kai, the child who held neither
fire nor water.

The Great River raised me in the twisted roots of the
kapok tree. She fashioned monkey brush vine and
bromeliad over the great twining limbs to hide me from
my mother's sight, but I have never been one to lie still. I
raced through the footpaths by day and climbed through
the treetops by night. But my new mother's eyes were
everywhere. She watched for me in the puddles along the
forest floor, in the drops of dew on the llama leaves; she
smiled at me from the droplets pooling in the skies. And
some days, she frowned at me from wooden bowls.

Lokemai, Namakaokahai called it. A village, she said.
Lokemai stands—or rather stoops—a shambling cluster of
refuge cobbled together from stone, wood, and palm
fronds, hovering in the silence of the lower jungle, just out
of reach of the river's floods. Mother Namakaokahai says
their men are skilled hunters, and it must be so. For my
brother, the jaguar, has never brought me meat from one.
Mother Namakaokahai warns me to stay away; she says
there is no room for me there, that Lokemai will not
fill me.

Nothing can fill Kai. Not fire, not water, not Lokemai.
But there are other things there, things I wish to see. So I
hide in the trees, I peer through the brush, I hover on the
edges of their village when the men leave for their great
hunts. And my mother frowns at me from wooden bowls
left out overnight to catch her offerings from the sky.

Qati, the women whisper when they see my footprints

or my path through the brush—the ghost child, the cursed. They grab their children's hands and murmur prayers to Mahuika, the fire goddess, to protect them from the ghost. They warn their daughters not to wander, lest I eat their souls beneath the cover of darkness. Their sons grab their spears and chase after me through the underbrush, all the way back to the muddy riverside. I let them chase me, for there is no fun in disappearing.

When I stumble home, muddy and smiling, Mother Namakaokahai scolds me, cleans me, kisses me, but she frowns. She tells me not to go, not to return, that the spear that pierces the flesh of my jaguar brothers will much more easily lacerate mine. She worries. I know she does. She worries because my lungs cannot accept the water, cannot make me hers in truth. She frets, and the river stews.

But she knows. She knows just like I do that I will return to Lokemai. She weeps at night, watches the twinkling stars gossip: Kai has found a treasure.

Mele. Dark of hair and bright of eye, a voice finer than the cotinga. The jungle announces this woman's presence with the tinkling of small bells gathered about her ankles. The sunlight dances with her, feathering over dark skin. Every morning, her mother paints her skin, her face, her arms, her legs, her stomach, her back and breasts, in colors that rival the parrot's feathers. Mele comes to Mother Namakaokahai's banks, dancing, carrying cracking clay pots, singing with the voice of heaven.

I ASKED her once if she feared Qati.

She said ghosts do not leave footprints.

Be careful little Mele, her mother warns, do not wander. Qati will take you; he will bring you harm.

She comes anyway. She comes to me, and I teach her my ways. I teach her to dig out the great roots of the taro tree and chew the meat of them. I teach her to choose the sweetest papaya leaves and suck the juice from their broken veins. I teach her not to touch the manchineel berries, for those will surely steal her small spirit from her.

And Mele, she teaches me to sing the song of the Great River.

She stands on the twisting roots of my kapok home, touching the surface of the water with painted toes. She smiles up at me, her hand in my muddy fingers, and when I bend close, she whispers the words into my ear.

"I dance before the Great River. In your great love, Namakaokahai, may you sing over me; gather me into your bosom, and I will worship thy great seas."

I listen to her worship, listen to the water gentle. Even when her eyes are far from us, when her seas rage against Mahuika instead of tenderly raining down on us, I wonder how Mother Namakaokahai cannot be pleased with us. How can she not adore Kai's treasure?

One day, I ask Mele this. I ask her what her heart thinks of this. She tells me that the people of Lokemai believe that once all the islands were one, that it was the warring of the two great sisters, Mahuika and Namakaokahai, that crumbled the land into pieces in the face of their wrath. It is why Maunakilauea, the great stone face, exists. It is where Mahuika built her home, to face the sea and all its fury. The people of Lokemai believe that Maunakilauea and its fire stand to protect them from the wrath of the sea. I hold Mele's delicate fingers and frown into the river. How does one tell their treasure that the truth is vastly different?

Mele tells me that she worships Namakaokahai to bring peace between the goddess and the people. She offers worship and prays that Namakaokahai's rage will subside, that my new mother will not leave their offering bowls empty. Mele leans her head against my shoulder, tells me how her people are starving. The sea rages against Maunakilauea's great stone face. Their people drown in Namakaokahai's seas trying to cook their meat on the stone face, and their gardens have ceased to grow, for Namakaokahai sends no rain. She fears for their lives, Mele whispers. She fears her worship will be for naught.

My treasure looks to me for reassurance, searches my eyes for comfort and truth. Tears streak the paint on her face, and I bury my fingers in her hair and weep with her. I wish that her paint could only be ruined by the cracks brought on by smiles and sunshine.

Come to Lokemai, Mele begs me. Come and teach my people to survive. Namakaokahai will smile on the place where you thrive. She begs, though we both know it cannot be so. For the spear that ends the jaguar's life will offer no mercy on mine.

Instead, I tell her, "Kekahai la e ho'omaka hou."

When the sounds of night gather in our ears, Qati guides Mele back to Lokemai, leaving behind a single set of footprints for the great hunters to find.

Every day I pray. Every day I beg my mother to turn from her anger, to save these people, but she refuses. My little Kai, she tells me, how can you understand? Have you ever been a mother? No, you cannot know what my sister has done. She strokes my hair and tries to soothe my distress in the night's gentler waters. But we both know there can be no forgiveness.

Mother Namakaokahai spends her days away from the river, her seas crashing against Maunakilauea's strong sides, valiant, berating darkness in the face of her sister's flames. I spend my days watching over Lokemai. I watch with my treasure as wobbling skeletons carry the bodies of their loved ones on stretchers to rest in the Great River. Mele says the cool water drives the spirits of sickness away.

Day after day more bodies are brought, laid out on Mother Namakaokahai's banks, sweating in the cold water until their teeth chatter and loved ones carry them home. Mele grieves deeply, but her mother will not allow her near the sick ones, will not allow her to the water to worship. So I take her to a safe place, downstream. There, she dances, sings, prays, weeps in the rushing waters, her muscled legs braced so Namakaokahai does not carry her away, as if she does not know that I would not let her.

Qati lurks on the riverbanks, her people say. He has brought the sickness upon them. He knows each body, each face, each breath taken by those he has cursed. They spit on my footprints, throw stones at my shadow, when Aukelenuiaiku gathers their loved ones into the great beyond.

The stars gossip when Mother Namakaokahai's spirit does not return from the seas to the river. They whisper that Kai, the empty one, will leave her for his treasure. And

I lie awake at night in my den of roots, knowing it cannot be so.

And so, the days pass. The sisters warring, the lovers grieving, the village chasing after shadows and ghosts. But Mele comes to me, every day, every day. Until one day, she does not.

The first days, I watch for her. Perhaps, I think, her mother has hidden her away. But the men hunt the forests for Qati, seeking justice, promising death, and it grows harder to hide. Beneath the cover of darkness, at the change of their guard, I slip gifts into Mele's offering dish. Taro root, papaya leaf, small stones and shells from the sea. Don't give up, I whisper to the empty wooden bowl. Return to Kai, return to me.

On the fifth day, I watch her mother wail, tear great handfuls of hair from her head, and trample my gifts into the ground. Then, I watch the water.

It is the eighth day when her mother brings her, on a stretcher woven from my papaya leaves. Mele lies pale, silent, quaking, and her body looks smaller, delicate. Her bones stick out at odd angles, stretching her skin, naked of its intricate paint design. Her mother ties her to the stretcher, and lays her on the shore, peering anxiously at the water and I peer with her. I wonder, does she see that Mother Namakaokahai is not there?

It is a long while before Mele's mother leaves her side, a bare moment when she disappears into the brush, leaving the stretcher tied in the shallows of the river. But moments are all Qati needs. The mud squelches beneath my knees when I drop beside her, and the Great River runs cold, so cold. How can such cold drive the sickness away?

When I touch Mele's face, my hand leaves behind streaks of mud. It should not look so garish against her skin, but my chest tightens around my breaths. Come back to me, treasure, I will her silently. She does not answer, does not smile, does not open her eyes to see me, but she breathes. She breathes.

My arms shake when I slide them beneath the wet leaves and gather her into my chest. I imagine the stars, their gossip, if I snatched her away from Aukelenuiaiku's grasp and carried her away, back to the kapok den covered in its monkey brush vine and bromeliad. Would Mother Namakaokahai return and bless us if I begged?

No, I think. My mother is too busy. Too busy seeking after her revenge, a revenge I cannot understand.

"Kekahai la e ho'omaka hou," I whisper to her, my Mele, my song. Another day. Another day to rise again.

Tears crawl down my face, the taste of them bitter and cutting in my mouth. The sound of them brings vengeance. Her mother screams and screams, her words a stream of fury, a great noise, like the fire that comes from Mahuika's hands and Maunakilauea's mouth. She stoops in the mud and picks up stones, hurling them into my body along with her screams.

Scuttling backward on all fours, I snarl. Blood dripping down my face stains the gaze from which I see her and the stone that my hand curls around. I could throw it, I could end her. The same way Mother Namakaokahai dreams of ending Mahuika. Mele's mother runs with fragile, weak steps for her daughter.

That is when the hunters come. Not sons with their small spears and excited snarling. These are the wolves among pups. Men larger than Qati, larger and stronger. A stone against these spears will do nothing.

The earth shakes behind me when they run, silent and ready, on the edges of my sight. My one eye does not see through the blood filling it; the other burns through its tears. But we run, hunters and ghost, the underbrush parting before us. Splinters snatch at my feet in the dry earth, the gympie bush sheds its poison barbs in my hands, my arms, my thighs and knees. What will the stars say this time? Kai, the empty boy, flees—with only a stone to protect him. The waves will not gather at his command, the flames will not burn. So here runs Kai, the ghost boy chased by man.

They chase and chase, all the way to the end of the river, to the path where man crosses from the Great River to the mountain, and it is there I lose them, hiding myself in the darkness of the jaguar's den until dark. My brothers bury me among them, in the heaving pile of their bodies as they rest. They comfort me; they say, "Man will not hunt what he cannot eat."

When darkness falls and the jaguars leave their den to hunt, I track with them, following the sheen of their glossy coats, letting it lead me home to the kapok tree on stumbling limbs. They follow behind me, their slim bodies covering the trail I leave. And then, once I am led safely back to my own den, they retreat.

Tossing and turning, my head aching, I lay in the cool wet mud of my den, shaking. The comfort so easily attained resting between the warm bodies of my brothers has left me. There is no silken fur, no deep easy breath to provide the warmth, the stability, the tenderness that none but they can grant me. Back and forth, like the leaves in the wind, I roll and writhe, thinking of my treasure, dying. And so, I rise and step out among the roots, staring into the shattered moonlight reflecting through the trees on the Great River's surface.

I peer up at the sky, dark but for that moon. The stars have ceased their twinkling, shrouded themselves. They sob, they cry, the treasure, the treasure lies dying. And my heart echoes their mourning.

How can I sleep, knowing my treasure lies suffering? How can anyone sleep? Why does the jungle not bow low, as broken as me? Can they not understand what they stand to have lost? I lean between the roots of the great kapok, shielded from the wind by its weathered skin. How can Mother Namakaokahai stay away at a time like this? How can she allow such suffering?

"Mother?" I ask her. "Do you know how you hurt me?"

She does not answer, her spirit far from home. I squeeze the stone which marred me tighter in my palm, then draw my arm back with a jaguar's scream and hurl it into her surface. It is the only way I know to share my pain with her.

It is there, collapsed between the roots, that Mother Namakaokahai finds me the next morning. Her face is bright and clear in the face of the sun, and she gathers me patiently into her arms. Salty water cleans my wounds, scalds away the mud, blood, and sting of the gympie leaves. Mother Namakaokahai soothes the jaguar screams from my throat with gulps of her essence, until my fragile body casts it back up.

"My child," she whispers, her icy fingers carrying me

back to my den beneath the kapok, "is one human so important?"

I search those pelagic eyes and answer her with the only truth I can find in the maw of her cool, forgiving darkness: "She fills me in all the places I am empty."

This time, it is my mother who cries.

Three days I lie beside her in the soothing darkness of my den. Mother Namakaokahai whispers that my heart has tried to kill me, that it rests torn apart inside me. She grieves over me, Kai, her poor empty boy. But the sickness in my heart gives birth to something new, something strong, something human: a plan.

When at last I am strong enough, I wake and I crawl into the Great River's arms and sink. She is gentle with me, her arms gathering me close against her chest, and I breathe, harsh bubbles escaping when the water will not fill me. Mother Namakaokahai guides me back to the surface, kisses my face, whispers, "Kekahai la e ho'omaka hou." She calls me her little one, her Kai, her son.

Lying on the bank between the kapok roots, I open my eyes to see her face. "I have felt it, my mother," I tell her. "I have felt the great rage."

Mother Namakaokahai clenches icy fingers around mine. "Mahuika," she says her sister's name with all the emptiness I feel inside of me. "She took my treasure." Her voice breaks like the trees dying in her forest, cracks and tumbles into my ears. "My husband. My children. All of it."

I squeeze her hands in my own and reply, "Then we shall take hers. We shall end this."

And when my mother, Namakaokahai, the Great River, smiles, it is a jagged cutting thing.

To save Lokemai, to bring back my Mele from the reach of Aukelenuiaiku's earthen palms, I must restore things to their rightful place.

Mele's prayers must be answered.

And so I tell this plan to Mother Namakaokahai. "Bring me up to the great stone face of Maunakilauea. I will meet my mother there, and I will bring you her fire."

Mother Namakaokahai frowns, the same frown she gives me from Lokemai's now empty bowls. "Can you not understand, my child?" she asks. "Mahuika's power is not in the mountain."

"Give me the secret then of where I may find Mahuika's power," I say. "So we may be rid of this war forever."

Mother Namakaokahai smiles, wearily. She smoothes my hair and retreats to the edge of the bank, watching me. "Aia ka mana o ke ola i na lima."

I gaze up into the canopy, at the sunlight through the spaces in the branches. What will the stars say tonight? Will they speak of Mele's death? Will they speak of mine? How long until they leave the sky, moving on from an island as desolate and empty as I am?

When I stand, the jungle stills around me; the morning sky aches with the weight of my decisions. "Great River, take me to the mountain." There is a grimace, a bearing of foamy teeth, before Mother Namakaokahai surges forward and plunges me into the racing of her waters. Never before and never again will the stars whisper of a river that flows upstream.

Mother Namakaokahai lifts me, long enough for my lungs to gather breath, here and there throughout our trek, her icy cold surrounding my muscles. In her arms, I lie achy, weighted, waiting, until at last, she places me upon the base of the mountain. "This is as far as I may take you," she says, placing a kiss upon my forehead. "When you gather the flames, bring them to me and I will destroy them. We will be rid of this fire forever." Then, she disperses in the face of the great mountain and trickles out to sea.

THE MOUNTAIN GROWS HIGHER with every step that I climb, higher and higher, into the clouds. Soot and stone crumble around me, and heat from Maunakilauea's face warms my shaking skin. But it is not the icy cold of the Great River that chills me, for that has passed from my limbs long ago. No, it is this, this realization: that I go before Mahuika, the great warrior, the wife of Aukelenuiaiku, the slayer of Mother Namakaokahai's treasures, her children. I go before Mahuika, the goddess who fed her empty son to the equally empty jaws of the Great River. I go before Mahuika, and I do not know what I will find there.

WHEN AT LAST I have surpassed the clouds and Mother Namakaokahai's seas are far out of my sights, the great stone mouth gapes before me, and in the steaming hush of Maunakilauea's breath, stands Mahuika, queen of the mountain, bathed in reflections of red. The great flames wrap themselves around her fingers, spreading up her elbows, flicking and eating at the charred and bleeding skin beneath. Maunakilauea's fire breath gathers around her feet. Mahuika does not wear paint like the people who worship her, who believe she protects them; she does not need it, for she is burning.

———

"WHO COMES BEFORE MAHUIKA, queen of the mountain?" Her voice echoes smooth and crackling, like the flame itself, from inside Maunakilauea's face, and it is as if she does not even open her mouth. But, I remind myself, her power does not come from the great mountain.

"Kai, child of the Great River comes," I say.

The great warrior queen laughs and Maunakilauea's breath sputters, bubbles with the sound. But her power does not come from the great mountain. "Namakaokahai has no children." She lifts a burning fist to the air and smiles, and my heart bumps, jumps, like Maunakilauea's boiling breath.

"It is true," I tell her. "Mother Namakaokahai's children are no more. Your great mountain has carried them into Aukelenuiaiku's arms."

"Then I ask again," her voice births itself from the crackling, writhing flames around her and her lips lie still. "Who comes before Mahuika, queen of the mountain?"

Her eyes are filled with soot, the same soot that grinds before her blackened teeth, but they spark and bloom with flashes of golden, raging fire. Her power does not come from the great mountain.

"You cast me into the Great River, for I was empty," I reply. Mahuika's flames sputter and lessen, the glow in her eyes dimming. "And the Great River spat me out, the same way its seas spit upon you." Mahuika's skin is burned, swollen, bleeding flesh.

"Keiki ha'aha'a," she murmurs and her fingers flex at her sides. My empty one, my low child, that is what she calls me. I nod and the queen of the mountain closes her eyes. One heartbeat, two, three. Then, fiery eyes flash open, the only black to be seen the narrow, tiny stone in their center. "Why has Keiki ha'aha'a come?" She asks.

"Mother Namakaokahai kills Kai's treasure." These are the words I give her. "I have come to you, the great goddess of the mountain, to end her."

Mahuika huffs, a great barking laugh, and Maunaki-lauea's breath leaps in a watery wave of fire behind it. "Do you think, Keiki ha'aha'a, that your mother has not tried? It is not such a simple task to kill the sea."

"The sea is not the Great River's power," I tell her. "I know the heart of her, a place deep within the forest. Give me the gift of your flame, my mother. I will carry it into the jungle and end her for you."

Mahuika smiles, a blackened, gaping thing, and sweeps her hand elegantly toward Maunakilauea's maw, indicating the rising, writhing breath. "By all means, my son. Take it."

But Mahuika's power is not in the mountain. I gesture, holding out my hand, and return to her the words that Mother Namakaokahai had given me: "Aia ka mana o ke ola i na lima"— The power of life is in the hands.

Mahuika's flames sputter, snap at the tips of her fingers, this time in her right hand, and I know this is where she hides them. Her treasures, her flame, the five fingers. Her raging eyes narrow at me; then she tips back her head in a great laugh that booms through the crater of Maunaki-lauea's mouth and sends her liquid breaths hurtling into the cloudy skies.

"Keiki ha'aha'a is wise," my mother replies. When I do not answer, my mother steps forward to join me at the edge of Maunakilauea's lips. She towers above me, regal even with her burns. "Very well then, my empty son. I will give you this fire, and you will destroy the Great River where it is born."

Gently, Mahuika reaches out and places a small golden flame in my open palm. A serpent's hiss escapes my lips and I shake away the pain it leaves, the small bleeding burn in the palm of my hand dissipating as the flame falls into the clouds and is gobbled up.

"Ack," Mahuika scowls, cross, as her smallest flame, given from her fifth finger, vanishes from sight. "Did Keiki ha'aha'a think the flame would not burn him?"

"I did not know," I answer her. Mahuika shakes her head, frowning until the singed hairs above her brows meet in the center of her face. She flicks her wrist and from her fourth finger, another flame alights.

"Take this flame," she says. "And this time, Keiki ha'aha'a do not be so forgetful."

Steeling my palm for the burn of the flame, I allow Mahuika to place it in my palm. The flames lick at my skin, catch at the bleeding surface where its brother did, and I turn away from my mother, my steps a hurried thing, slip-ping and sliding through the stones and soot and dirt down Maunakilauea's face to meet Mother Namakaoka-hai's waves at the place where the sea meets the ground.

Standing in her presence, her icy spray against

Maunakilauea's stone face, I offer up the burning brother, trembling. Mother Namakaokahai bends over me and takes the golden flame in her hands, crushes and swallows it into the dark abyss of her. Then, she soothes the burn with a kiss on my palm.

"Three more," she whispers. "Be brave, my child."

I close my eyes and let her cool breath spread over me, prepare for the great climb back to Maunakilauea's mouth. "Kekahi la e ho'omaka hou," I answer. Mother Namakaokahai smiles, a tense, cutting thing.

And then, I climb back to the surface. Mahuika waits there, impatient, frowning. I bow down to one knee and beg, "Forgive me, great queen of the mountain, but the stones on the mountainside are loose and I have fallen. Your flame was crushed by the stones. Forgive your son, for he is clumsy."

Mahuika puffs a great breath of steam into the air and stomps her feet in Maunakilauea's breath as she comes to me. The liquid breath splatters, stinging my shins and thighs. With a flick of her wrist, Mahuika births a flame from her third finger. "Take this flame, Keiki ha'aha'a," she says. "And do not be so ungainly."

So it is again, that I make the trek down the great mountain's face, and this time, Mother Namakaokahai meets me higher up the side of the mountain, at the place where Maunakilauea s belly begins to narrow just beneath the clouds. Like the first, she swallows Mahuika's second flame, and she smiles patiently. "Two more flames, my Kai," she says. "Then her fire will be no more."

I peer up into the sky, shadowed thick with heavy white clouds. Can the stars see me now? Do they know what Kai, the empty child, is doing? Will they sing this story into the night? "Two more," I echo and I trek back up the mountain.

Once more, Mahuika meets me at the face of the mountain. With a great snarl, she snaps her hand and I am not certain if it is skin or flame that cracks across my face, sending me to my knees before her. "Tell me, clumsy Keiki ha'aha'a, why have you returned to me this time?"

Maunakilauea's breath bubbles, splatters, stinging the backs of my hands and neck when I press my face to her stone and soot, bowing low before my mother's wrath. "Forgive me, great queen of the mountain, but the clouds have grown greedy. They have trapped me on the mountain, and in my confusion and blindness, your third flame was eaten by the great sea. Forgive your son, for he is inattentive."

Mahuika heaves a great sigh and her bloody hands lift me to kneeling before her. With a flick of her wrist, she births a fourth flame from her second finger and places the golden child in my palm once again. "Take this flame, inattentive Keiki ha'aha'a," she says. "And this time, do not be so distrait."

So it is, a third time, I descend the mountain's face, and this third time, Mother Namakaokahai meets me even higher upon Maunakilauea's face, near the smooth cliffs of her throat. She gobbles up the fourth flame and praises her empty child. "This is the last one, my beautiful child. The final flame and your mother will be no more."

"I know," I tell her, and I trudge, a final time, up the face of the mountain.

Mahuika waits at the top, screaming her fury at my

arrival. "Keiki ha'aha'a, why have you returned to me this time?"

"Forgive me, great queen of the mountain," I say, raising my eyes to her, stiffening my body in the face of her final leaping flame. "For I have sinned."

Mahuika's eyes narrow, consumed by soot, weakened by the loss of her power. The power of life is in the hands, and Mahuika holds only one flame left. Surging forward, she bears down on her son, a single flame building larger and larger, Maunakilauea's breath bubbling higher and higher, forcing me to the edge of her lips.

"It would have been better," Mahuika says, grabbing her hand in my hair, "if Keiki ha'aha'a was never born."

A jaguar's smile, full of teeth and fury, is all I have to offer her when I grab a hold of her burning arm in return. "My name is Kai," I answer. Then, Kai, the empty child, rears his head forward and eats his mother's final flame, taking her finger with it.

Mahuika's scream splits the skies and shakes the earth, and when she releases her hand from my hair, I turn and throw myself down the side of Maunakilauea's face. I can see her. I can see the dark, grasping arms of Mother Namakaokahai's seas rising to meet me. As I crash into them, plunged into the crushing depths of her, I wonder how the stars will sing of the burning inside me. And when Mother Namakaokahai's cool arms surround me, I close my mouth and refuse to breathe.

The waves crash, pushing and pulling around me, and my lungs ache and burn. I shiver and shudder, limbs heavy but thrashing. I am filled, for the first time, with fire, and it burns me from the inside out. When Mother

Namakaokahai throws me onto the cliffside shore, I land, broken, screaming.

"Give it to me," Mother Namakaokahai begs urgently. "Give me the flame, Kai. I will destroy this; I will end her." Great booming, hissing, and wailing come from the clouded mountain, and it covers up my "no." It does not shield me from Mother Namakaokahai's horror or Mother Mahuika's rage, nor from the flames inside me.

And so, I turn and run. Run. For that is what I, Kai, the empty boy, the child of the Great River, the Qati of the jungle, do best. I flee over the rugged terrain, away from the river, away from the mountain, back toward the forest, to Lokemai, to Mele—the goddesses of both fire and water raging after me.

I can feel it, the hot breath of Maunakilauea pouring down the mountainside. Even in the brief glances back at Maunakilauea's face, I see the liquid breath pouring down her rocky face, carrying my mother's screams. Spilling after me, it covers everything; it burns everything away. And Mother Namakaokahai is nowhere to be seen.

The rugged earth breaks around me beneath the force of Maunakilauea's shaking and it gobbles up her breath, but there is more, always more, and the moment I hit the forest, it is breaths away from consuming all of us.

But something new is coming. I feel it in the shift of the wind, the darkening face of the clouds, the hushed calm of the river and seas. Mother Namakaokahai is coming; she is coming to protect me.

And then, as I have not seen in years, the skies split apart and the seas open up, this time from above, emptying themselves over the islands, battling with Maunakilauea's breath until her fire has turned to stone and the angry rain, the howling wind, the shaking earth, and two sisters' screams are all that are left.

The vicious, heavy rain stings my burns, pounds my shoulders, turns the rugged, dry terrain into mud. Trees slide, plants ripped from their places, and animals rush from their dens for higher ground, safer shelter. And in all of this, the river rises, rages, her mud and water grasping me as my stumbling feet carry me closer and closer to the rattling, crumbling village of Lokemai.

At the edge of Lokemai, the men have retreated. Their spears lie broken in the mud, and the rising river licks at my heels. Mother Namakaokahai calls for me through the torrents of rain and I can see them. An entire village of people, huddled and covering each other beneath the collapsing palm frond roof of Mele's home. I can see her, gripped tightly in her parents' arms, pale and still, sleeping, amidst her people's fear.

I wonder if she knows, her prayers for rain have been answered.

Then, behind me, Mother Namakaokahai rears her face through the rain, her form building between the falling and the rising waters. When I turn to meet her, her face is all confusion, all darkness, all rage.

And when I speak, I say the only thing that I can: "Mother, you must stop this. You will destroy them all." Her rain spews angrily, forcefully from the sky, and I raise my hands to touch her face, the burned palms aching beneath the weight of her. "Mother," I ask her, "will you take my treasure from me?"

Then, it stops. The river retreats to its bed, but the

earth continues its shaking and Mother Namakaokahai's form weeps in the gentle continuing rain. "Give me the flame, Kai," she begs. "Let me end this evil thing." Her hands clasp my shoulders, shake.

When I place my hands against her cheeks and my forehead against her face, I shake my head and the rain heaves harder against the earth once again. "My mother," I whisper gently. "I have tricked you. Can you not see this?"

"I can," she says. "I can."

"My mother," I ask her, "can you not see that we are safe now? There is no more power in Mahuika's hands."

Mother Namakaokahai sobs and her fingers hold my face, the same as I hold hers. "You must release this flame," she begs. "I did not want this for you. I did not want you to hold this fire that will hurt you."

"I will," I promise her. "I know this. But you must promise me something, my mother." When she looks at me, her clear but clouding depths cause shivering on my skin, but it does not ease the burning within. "We must take back our treasures," I tell her. "We must protect our people."

"My treasures are gone," Mother Namakaokahai answers me.

"My mother," I answer, "is Kai, not your son?" In answer, her great arms surround me and my mother weeps until the skies can give no more, and Mahuika's screams and the earth's shaking are silenced. Then, she hovers there, in the puddles, the streams, the risen river that meets me at the edge of the village once more.

And we stand there together, in the still silence, listening to the steady drip, drip, drip of her in the trees.

After a time, when I can stand the burning no more, I turn away from my mother. Trudging through the mud toward the single shelter housing the people of Lokemai, I bend to pick up Mele's empty offering bowl.

"Qati," her mother whispers fearfully when I step inside the broken shelter and kneel there in the doorway.

"Ghosts do not leave footprints," I answer her. Then, with a flick of my wrist, I birth Mahuika's single flame from my fingertips. It fills the wooden bowl, leaving me with a raw, weary emptiness. "I am Kai, son of the Great River, and I bring you gifts. I bring you rains from Sister Namakaokahai to grow your crops, and I bring you flame from Sister Mahuika to warm your bodies and cook your meats. Together, they will drive away sickness and fill you with good things. Share these gifts among your people and know that Qati has done this for his treasure, Mele."

Then, like the crabs on the rocky cliffs, I scuttle backward through the mud and back to my mother's side, leaving them the single flame, praying it will spread and last long enough to give the people of Lokemai many, many good things.

Together on this day, my mother and I return to our home. Mother Namakaokahai returns to her source in the small pool and remains there with me, her son, beneath the roots of the kapok tree, gathering rat's tail to heal my many burns.

———

IT IS many days before I hear her.

I hear her first—in the bells, their tinkling as she dances

through the forest, then in her voice, singing to me, as it always has, the Great River's song. She stops there, standing on the root of the kapok tree, and the paint on her face cracks when she smiles.

She returns to me, just as I left her, only stronger, fuller. But I do not return to my beloved the same. My skin bears scars, splatters, and great disfigurement across my face, my hands, my legs. But Mele places her palms on my cheeks and says, "The stars sing to me of fire."

"Do they sing also to you of water?"

Mele places her lips on mine then and only smiles.

———

SO YOU SEE, children, today, a great river crashes through the forest, its mighty hands tearing stone and limb. It winds its paths through the jungles and spills its waters gently in Lokemai's fields. And while the seas yet rage upon the great stone face of Maunakilauea, Lokemai knows its true protector.

This day, children, the stars sing many songs. They sing of Sister Namakaokahai who pours her gifts out on the island people. They sing of Sister Mahuika who lost her flame and of how the islanders stole the heart of her. They sing of Kai, the child who grew into a man, into a great chief of Lokemai, lord of the sea, lover of Mele—the son who was never empty, for he had been filled with his mother's love. And they sing of his mother, his true mother, who was glad her treasure had been born.

WHEN THE NIGHT LEFT

BY SAVANNA ROBERTS

T he girl who painted sunsets hated night.
     Or rather, she hated the man who brought
nights.

Nyx's son was cocky with his punctuality, arriving
every day at the exact same time to wash the paintings she
created with Helios in inky black. He had no regard for her
art, no regard for the pink and golden hues she slaved over.
She doubted he even had a soul to appreciate it.

Helios told her it was the man's job. It was the way the
world worked. But to Dysis, the nights were stifling and
endless. If one were to live forever in the sky, they should
be allowed the warmth of the sun, the sight of the sunrise
and sunset for more than thirty minutes each, before the
chilly void engulfed them.

She put up with it for decades, for centuries, awaiting
dusk with dread, nighttime with terror. Until she decided
she couldn't do it, that she needed something to distract
her from her fear.

She tried sleeping in the field with Helios's horses, but

the animals were wild and never stayed in one spot. They left her feeling more alone than when she was by herself.

She approached her sisters, but the Daughters of the Evening laughed at her. "Foolish girl," they tittered. "Why do you let follies dance through your head? The sky is always the sky."

She even lowered herself to the sun god's bed, hoping it would drive away the nightmares. The sun god's bronze chest dripped sweat onto his sheets, his curls messy and clinging to his forehead, and he leaned on muscular forearms next to her, an amused grin on his face. "A sky nymph should not fear the heavens," Helios admonished. "It is your home."

No matter what she tried, the nights still came. Nyx's son brought them with a flick of his wrist, with a smirk that could rival the sun god's. Sometimes his mother came with him and praised his work, and Dysis would suffocate as her hand became a mere shadow in front of her face, as she was reminded that no matter how hard she worked, how beautiful she painted, she was still alone.

It was her and blackness stretching to the end of time, and that was all it would ever be.

SHE SANK INTO DEPRESSION, into a pit of dread that swallowed her away from her sisters and Helios and the gods themselves. And she stewed as her dread turned to rage, as her brushstrokes became stabs of her paintbrush in the sky – red and orange and furious.

One day, when Nyx's son arrived exactly on time, she

stood there waiting for him, arms crossed over her chest. "Why do you hate color?" she demanded of him. They had never spoken before, not once, but as her sister nymphs turned Helios's horses loose in their pasture, she found she couldn't keep her mouth shut a moment, a decade, a *century* longer.

The man of nights gave her a lazy grin. "Black has more mystery than your pretty colors ever will."

He tugged one of her locks of golden hair before spreading his arms wide and drowning her sunset in a mass of darkness.

He did not give her a moment to admire her work one more time before he washed it out. He did not even apologize before he disappeared in his blackness.

———

THE GIRL who painted sunsets and the man of nights went on this way until a full millennia had passed. They did not age because they were the only ones who could paint the skies. It was lonely work, but they never put aside their differences to become friends. The girl who painted sunsets wanted nothing to do with the monster that ruined them. The man of nights thought his work was above the girl, so he didn't want anything to do with her either.

That's when the Fates decided to intervene.

As the centuries continued to pass and Dysis was belittled for desiring companionship, and Nyx's son realized what a lonely world it was, an unexpected thing began to happen.

The man of nights began to look forward to seeing the

sunset every evening. The colors made him happy. The girl who painted them made him smile.

"It's Dysis, right?" he finally asked her one evening, Helios having revealed the nymph's name to him at his request.

She rubbed one of the shimmering horses' necks and didn't look at him. "Yes."

"I'm Cepheus."

This time, she did meet his gaze, and the raw pain in her eyes made his breath catch. "Why do you think I care?"

This conversation seemed inevitable to be their last.

He still had to wash her colors away, but on some days, his heart would break when he saw the depths of sadness in her eyes, and he would let her admire her creation for a few moments more. But it did little to help her and nothing to spark an understanding, a relationship, between them.

Every night, after the man had washed the color from the sky, he would take care to arrange the stars in new patterns, hoping to catch Dysis's attention. The mortals below called the stars a *phenomenon*. The girl who painted sunsets didn't notice.

More centuries passed with Cepheus continuing to soften his heart toward the girl and create glistening masterpieces for her.

And more centuries passed where Dysis continued to harden her heart toward the man's advances and sell her body and soul to someone she thought might save her from the night. But century after century passed with both still suffering, bound tight in a destiny that Cepheus raced towards while Dysis desperately ran away.

THE MAN of nights began to get desperate. He could not live in a world of loneliness and heartache any longer. He could not stand the way the girl's shoulders hunched lower and lower, as she retreated further into herself, every time he washed her colors away. He could not stand creating the night and aligning patterns of stars if even his small gifts of light went unnoticed; if his creations tormented her so.

At the end of a masterful sunset, he met the girl and fell to his knees before her. "What must I do to earn your affection? What must I do to take away your pain? That is all I desire in the world."

The girl who painted sunsets thought for a moment, and when she looked down at the man of nights, her eyes were devoid of warmth.

"Leave my sunsets alone. Give up your art. Only then will I appreciate you."

The man of nights was stunned to hear such a proposal, but nonetheless, he thought it over. Giving up his passion for inky blackness and intricate constellations would involve misery. But surely he could bear it if the girl gave him a chance, if he didn't have to feel lonely anymore. Surely he could bear it if it meant healing the soul he'd been breaking to pieces for centuries.

Cepheus rose to his feet, cupped her fair face in his hands, and kissed both of her cheeks. "Consider it done." And he left, for he had no work to do, no passionate masterpiece to create. He took what he presumed was her affections with him.

AT FIRST, Dysis relished in his absence. She wouldn't mind sending him her affections, telling him whatever he desired to hear, since he wasn't trapping her in an endless void. She'd been whispering lies to Helios and other gods for as long as she could remember to chase away her fears. She no longer had to be afraid of the night or the loneliness that clenched her bones and kept her mind from sleeping.

But the hours grew long. Where once the masterpiece of night would have been, she had to stay up and paint so the sky wouldn't be devoid of color until the morning.

A weariness so deep and heavy, even for an immortal, settled in her bones.

She began to hate the man of nights for leaving her in this predicament. This had to be part of some deeper, more awful plan. If he had really wanted her affections, really wanted to heal her pain, he wouldn't have put her in this situation.

The days wore on. Dysis got sloppy with her paintings. Her creativity ebbed away. People were getting sick of the constant sunsets, sick of her.

"You paint like you're dying," Helios admonished. "Should Hades come collect you? Or perhaps Persephone won't have you – you would glow too brightly, brighter than her. Hades would take you to the Underworld and Persephone would spit you out."

"She taints the sunrise, she ruins the sunset," her sisters hissed when they thought she was too busy releasing the horses in the pasture to hear. "We can do better. Her follies have squandered our beauty."

And one day, while the girl cried as she tried to draw enough strength to weave colors in the sky in a new way – *"Will this loneliness ever end?", "Will this agony ever cease?", "I'm tired of being so afraid"* – she realized that her self-pity was foolishly misplaced.

The man of nights had not abandoned her to a horrible fate such as this. She had told him to go. And, because he loved her and so desired her affections in return, he had given up his own masterpieces to do as she wished. Because he'd longed to take away her pain, he'd given up the most important thing to him in hopes of healing her heart.

It was a revelation that stunned her, until the painting of the sky was forgotten. Her sisters screeched and flew to finish the sunset for her, but she ignored their antics.

Perhaps her fears could be conquered. Not by running to people who took advantage of her and her wary state of mind, but by forming a connection with someone who understood her, who was just as lonely as she was.

And the mortals below didn't want one kind of art. It wasn't in human nature to appreciate Picasso and no one else, to appreciate sculptures and not sketches. They wanted variety: darkness and stars, colors and light, dark mysteries and bright fantasies. They wanted something more than what her own paintings could convey.

The girl who painted sunsets realized she missed the man's art too. Every star he hung in the sky so she could still see in the void. Every constellation he created to try to draw her eye to his beauty. She'd taken it for granted before, thought him cocky. She hadn't realized…

She set down her paintbrush, dried her eyes, and then

called out to the man of nights. She called three times before he appeared.

"Yes?" Cepheus mumbled, head lowered to avoid her gaze.

"The stars," Dysis said. "Were they for me?"

Cepheus looked up. "All of them."

"Why?" The word was a whisper, for now she was less afraid of the nights and more afraid of being rejected by the man who created them.

Cepheus's eyes were midnight pools, the void itself, and yet she found she did not mind getting lost in them; not this time. "Because I love you, Dysis. And I am exhausted of our hatred. We are the only two in the world who paint the sky. We are the only two in the world who can understand one another. I'm afraid of being lonely. Does that not scare you too?"

Dysis's chest lurched with an unreleased sob, with the acknowledgement of his love, the feeling of being seen for the first time in the centuries she'd lived.

"I was wrong," she breathed when she controlled her voice enough to speak. "I was selfish and foolish. The world needs both of our art. *I* need your art. I need its stars and its mystery. I, too, grow weary of our hatred. I am afraid of being lonely. Paint for me and the mortals again, my love, and I hope to one day earn as much of your affection as you have mine."

The man of nights drew her to him and kissed both her cheeks again with tears in his eyes. "My darling, I will paint the most magnificent sky the world has ever seen in your honor."

The girl who painted sunsets was not sad to see her art

washed away this time. Instead, she sat back and marveled as the man of nights went to work, designing the sky as only he could, hanging the stars in intricate patterns that had never been crafted before. And when they lay down in the pasture to admire his art, Cepheus's arms wrapped tight around Dysis, neither were afraid because they had one another.

Decades after their union, the mortals would still call that night sky the prettiest to ever grace the earth.

MEET THE AUTHORS

Rosie Grymm - The Gumiho of Dragon River: Rosie Grymm is a young Christian writer who grew up travelling the world as a military kid. She developed her love of fairytales and mythology while taking family field trips to German castles and exploring Korean folk villages. Story-telling has always been a prominent part of her life. And when not writing, she can be found reading from her ever growing pile of books or planning her next travel adventure. She currently lives in Northern Illinois with her family and dog, Cinder(ella).

Hannah Carter - Of Underwoods and Underworlds: Hannah Carter is just a girl who loves to dream and write, and still wakes up every day hoping this will be the day she figures out she's secretly a mermaid. Her flash fiction pieces have been published by Go Havok, and two of her pieces were selected to be included in their Prismatic anthology. She also won a competition with her short story, "Lara." She currently has two published novellas, *Amir and the Moon* and *Seashells*. In addition to fiction, Hannah also has had over a dozen devotionals published in various magazines, as well as three devotions published in *Finding God in Anime*.

Connect with her through Instagram, Facebook, or her author website!

Abigail McKenna - The Breakriver Banshee: Abigail McKenna has been dreaming about magic since she was small, so now she weaves it into stories that are full of hope and the love of life. She can usually be found rereading an old favorite book, watching a mystery show, or dreaming about how to get her characters out of predicaments she put them in.

Mariella Taylor - Namakaokahai's Treasure: Mariella Taylor was raised on fairy lit paths somewhere between the backstreet alleys of Jackson, Mississippi, and the jazz infested avenues of New Orleans. Currently, she's settled in the open meadows of Iowa where the tulips grow thicker than the grass. She graduated with her terminal degree in Writing and Editing from University of Nebraska (Omaha) in 2018, and now she delegates her writing efforts to mentoring young authors, providing editing services to Indie writers, and grumbling at her uncooperative characters. She hopes one day to talk those characters into becoming part of a book.

Mariella can be reached at her email thefolded-world@gmail.com. You can also reach out to her through Instagram, Facebook, Goodreads, Pinterest, or on her blog.

 **Savanna Roberts - When the Night Left:** Savanna Roberts is a YA and NA author, freelance editor, wife, and proud mama of a spunky little girl and two sweet kitties. She's been writing seriously since she was ten years old, and she currently has seven books published and has written an article for *Introvert, Dear*, as well as collaborated on blog events with other writers. In her free time, she enjoys reading, adventuring with her husband and daughter, snuggling her cats, playing D&D, rooting for the Astros, and drinking chai.

For writing updates, book reviews, and more, you can check out her website: www.booksbysr.com

ABOUT THE PUBLISHER

SR Press is a small hybrid publishing house that offers traditional publishing services for Indie Authors. Specializing in Dystopian and Fantasy Young Adult/New Adult stories, we aim to make self-publishing more accessible, enjoyable, and successful for authors.

For more of our books or to view our author services, please visit our website at www.sr-press.com or follow us on the socials.